James Leasor was educated at The City [of London School and] Oriel College, Oxford. In World War [II he enlisted] into the Royal Berkshire Regiment [and served with the] Lincolns in Burma and India, where h[e spent four and a] half years. His experiences there stimulated his interest in India, both past and present, and inspired him to write such books as Boarding Party (filmed as The Sea Wolves), The Red Fort, Follow The Drum and NTR. He later became a feature writer and foreign correspondent at the Daily Express. There he wrote The One that Got Away, the story of the sole German POW to escape from Allied hands. As well as non-fiction, Leasor has written novels, including the Dr Jason Love series, which have been published in 19 countries. Passport to Oblivion was filmed as Where the Spies Are with David Niven. He died in September 2007.

www.jamesleasor.com

Follow on Twitter: **@jamesleasor**

A Week of
LOVE

BY

JAMES LEASOR

Being seven adventures of Dr Jason Love

Published by
James Leasor Publishing, a division of Woodstock Leasor Limited
81 Dovercourt Road, London SE22 8UW

www.jamesleasor.com

This is copyright material and must not be copied, reproduced, transferred, distributed, leased, licensed or publicly performed or used in any way except as specifically permitted by the publishers, as allowed under the terms and conditions under which it was purchased or as strictly permitted by applicable copyright law. Any unauthorised distribution or use of this text may be a direct infringement of the publisher's rights and those responsible may be liable in law accordingly.

First published 1969

This edition published 2014

© Estate of James Leasor 1969, 2014, 2020

For Ann

Contents

SUNDAY IN GIGLIO	The fourth sapele coffin
MONDAY IN PORTUGAL	Hero or heroin?
TUESDAY IN HOLLAND	The seventy-sixth face
WEDNESDAY IN SCOTLAND	Frozen asset
THURSDAY IN SPAIN	Five miles to the gallon
FRIDAY IN ENGLAND	Jewels from an empire crown
SATURDAY IN THE SURGERY	An echo from the past

SUNDAY in Giglio

The fourth sapele coffin

From where he sat, under the striped cafe awning, facing the crescent-shaped beach, the setting sun had turned Giglio's tiny harbour into a golden floor. Two small yachts bobbed at anchor, and a crowd of locals stood watching the last ferry of the day sail out through the harbour mouth towards Porto Santo Stefano. Someone tuned a guitar at an upper window; the single notes fell from it like drops of music on the umber evening air.

Dr Jason Love lit a Gitane. He was thinking of his friend Jackson and their long discussions during Jackson's last illness.

'I know you think the South of France is almost unbeatable - where the developers haven't ruined it, that is,' Jackson had said so often. 'But I spent some of my best years painting in Giglio. The developers haven't even heard of that island yet. So you really must go and see it before they do.'

Of course, he had said he would, but, of course, he never went; and now Jackson was dead, and to Love's surprise and embarrassment he had left his doctor £200 on condition that he spent it on a trip to Giglio.

Love had flown his Cord to France, and then drove across Europe. Now that great white beast was stabled in a garage in Porto Santo Stefano, an object of wonder and awe to the Italian mechanics. Love had crossed to Giglio in the ferry the previous day, and was staying in the splendid new Campese Hotel, all glass and terrazzo, on the far side of the island.

It was too soon yet to say whether he agreed with Jackson or not; certainly Giglio, with its medieval castle and look-out towers, its steep, winding roads and sudden rocky precipices slicing down to isolated, empty beaches, was the antithesis of the overcrowded Riviera.

He was there, of course, at the end of the season. Things might be different in August, but the only other visitors in his hotel were a handful of priests, with rooms along the corridor from him. They nodded pleasantly enough when they passed, but Love's Italian was infinitesimal, and he thought it possible that the priests knew as little English.

He ordered another Campari; the only thing he missed was his usual Bacardi rum and lime, but when in Rome (or not so far from Rome) etc. One drink led to another, and soon darkness was rolling in over the shimmering sea. He decided to eat at the pensione and then walk back over the spine of the island to the hotel. After two days' hard driving in a car nearly thirty years old, the exercise would do him good.

The night moths began to dance frantically around the fluorescent lights above his head as though they realized they only had hours to live. An unexpectedly chill breeze, a trailer for the mistral, blew in bleakly over the sea. Love shivered and decided that one unavoidable snag with a late holiday was that you felt you were somehow outstaying your welcome. There was in this a parallel with the whole human condition; you were living on borrowed time. Every day was shorter than the last, and every day the sun grew colder.

As though to disprove his thoughts, the patrone came out to him, with a menu as large as a theatre programme. For a start, they could offer the Signor a speciality of the region, suppa de pesca. And then a dozen scampi, skewered and grilled, with a bottle of the local white wine. Would the Signor care to stay to dinner? The Signor would and did.

Thus it was nearly ten o'clock when Love paid his bill and set off on the long climb back to his hotel. White clouds were already beginning to obscure the moon, and the harbour was deserted. Here and there a mooring rope creaked or a rising fish made a tiny splash of water. Love walked out of the port, between the little general store and the chemist, under the hand-painted sign for the Bahamas Underwater School. Behind the village, the road climbed sharply and the air felt sweet with the scent of night-blooming flowers.

He paused to look back over the peaceful scene. A few mosquitoes whined complainingly, and he heard a distant buzz from some heavy-winged moth. The rest was night and silence. Now that he was standing still, other tiny noises came alive; the intermittent clockwork whirr of crickets and cicadas, the rustle of a lizard on a leaf. Then the whining grew louder and more persistent. No moth could make such a noise; it must be coming from a group of stone huts on the roadside, farther up the hill.

He climbed up towards them, and the sound grew louder with every step he took. A slat of light shone out beneath an unpainted wooden door. Under the filtered moonlight, the road wound on upwards, empty as a dead man's eyes; behind him, the stone arm of the harbour wall cradled the sleeping yachts.

Love crossed to the door, and, feeling rather ashamed of his action (but what the hell, he was curious) he applied one eye to a knothole. As he did so, he wondered obliquely what excuse he could give if he saw another eye, looking out.

He didn't. Instead, on a floor almost ankle deep in sawdust, two men were cutting planks with a circular saw. In the background lay a front door, newly made for a house as yet unbuilt; then a chest of drawers, and a spindle-backed chair. The sharp smell of sweat and sapele wood blew out to him; obviously, they were working overtime in the local carpenter's shop.

Love looked through another hole that gave a better view of the rear of the workshop. There, a third man was screwing together several short planks, all about four feet long. Suddenly, Love realized with a shock what they were making; they were fashioning four tiny coffins, each just large enough to contain the corpse of a child.

Now who on a summer island night could possibly use four children's coffins, except four dead children? Had there been an epidemic, an accident that had wiped out a family, or was this just for some under-taker's stockroom?

Love walked on, his professional curiosity aroused, turning over possibilities in his mind. Two hundred yards away from the hut he stood to one side to let a small Fiat pass by. It passed and stopped. The driver wound down his window.

'Like a lift?' he asked in English.

'Nothing better,' said Love, thinking rather disappointedly, Is it so obvious I'm English? He had rather prided himself on his continental appearance in dark blue slacks, rope-soled sandals, and loose denim shirt.

They drove in silence, the night moths fluttering in their headlights.

'Come in and have a drink,' said Love, when they reached his hotel.

'Thank you, no,' replied the driver. 'I'm the local doctor, and it's bad for my reputation to breathe out alcohol.'

'I know all that,' said Love sympathetically. 'Because I'm a doctor on holiday. But at this hour, the surgery's surely over?'

'So it is. I'll bow to another medical opinion and prescribe myself a vodka.'

They sat on the terrace, and threw the ball of unimportant conversation back and forth for a few minutes.

'Tell me,' began Love, looking out at the sea, now the colour of pewter under the clouded moon. 'Have you had any deaths in the island recently?'

'Not this week,' replied the doctor. 'And by the grace of God, not next week, either.'

'No children?'

'Certainly not. Why do you ask?'

'Just curious,' said Love.

'We should have a few more children over here tomorrow,' the doctor went on, sipping his Masquers. 'We've got forty coming from an orphanage on the mainland. I believe their visit's being organized by some priests who are staying in this hotel. Some strange sect or other, but one that does a lot of good work, so I hear.'

He finished his Strega and looked at his watch.

'Must be off,' he said. 'If I stay any longer, there's a baby practically certain to arrive tonight. I feel it in the air. Thanks for the drink.'

Love watched the tail-lights of his little car die away in the warm darkness. The reception clerk had already gone to bed, so Love took his own key from the hook, and went up to his room.

Four small coffins, no small corpses, but a party of forty children due in the morning. Were these facts just coincidence - or something more?

His experience as an occasional agent for D.I.6, the British overseas Intelligence network, told him that in the shadowy world of crime and espionage there was no room for coincidences; only for consequences.

He locked his door, opened his suitcase, took out a small transistorized tape recorder and spoke for several minutes into its microphone. Colonel Douglas MacGillivray, the deputy head of D.I.6 in London, who controlled the movements of British agents abroad, had given this to him when he had called in on his way through London from his country medical practice in Somerset.

'We're thinking of issuing them to a number of our people,' MacGillivray had explained. 'Take this with you, and if anything crops up, try it. We want to see how it works in as many different situations and over as many different telephone systems as possible before we decide whether to go ahead or not.'

Sometimes, agents abroad had no time to go through the traditional rigmarole of coding messages which were routed to headquarters by roundabout means to minimize detection, possibly to Durban, then on to Delhi, and finally to London. Yet they could not risk speaking on an open telephone line in case their calls were tapped. For such emergencies, these tiny tape-recorders could provide a solution.

The agent recorded his message on the tape, then put in a telephone call to one of several apparently innocuous London firms (from an importer's near London Bridge, to a fruit wholesaler's in Covent Garden). Each agent had his own recognition phrases (which were constantly being changed) and this alerted the London office to expect a secret call, and not a genuine business inquiry. The agent would then play over his message at a pre-arranged and immensely high speed. The result would be gibberish, unintelligible to anyone listening in - and almost unbreakable as a code. To decipher it, the London listening post would simply play it back at normal speed.

The Russians had used this method for radio messages for a long time. The Krogers, alias the Cohens, who had been jailed in 1961 for twenty years at the Old Bailey over the British Naval Secrets case, had actually embedded one such machine in the concrete foundations of their house in Ruislip and used it when they transmitted their radio messages to the Soviet Secret Service HQ in the Lubyanka Prison building in Moscow. But it had not been used over the telephone system to any great extent, and here was a chance to see how the thing worked.

Love picked up his telephone, gave the sleepy operator a Fleet Street number in London, ostensibly the office of a news agency. At that hour, the lines were clear; within ten minutes he was giving his identification phrase. Then he held the tape recorder against the receiver and played his message.

The London duty officer said: 'This line is so bad, I'll have to ring you back. Please repeat your hotel number.'

Love knew from this reply that his message had been received clearly and would be decoded; if reception had been patchy, he would have been asked for his home number. So much for that; he reloaded his recorder and thankfully went to bed.

He was awakened at half-past eight by the purr of his Juvenia alarm watch. There was also some commotion outside in the corridor. He opened the door and saw eight priests in black walking in file towards the marble staircase. The last one glanced towards Love's open door, and when he saw him, made the sign of the cross; Love nodded a greeting.

As he watched him go, he wondered what it was that jarred his mind about him. Something was slightly out of character, like a picture viewed through the wrong pair of spectacles. It was not until he had finished breakfast on his balcony that he realized what it was. The fingers he had raised in the blessing had been stained with nicotine. Surely no member of a religious sect in Italy would smoke so heavily?

Love spent the morning under a sun umbrella, writing atrociously-coloured postcards to some of his more favoured patients. At eleven o'clock, he heard the ululation of the double horns on the blue single decker bus arriving from the port. It pulled a plume of dust along the coast road and turned into the parking space behind the hotel.

The driver cut his engine, jumped down and ran towards the Campese. His passengers streamed in after him, all talking loudly together, gesticulating to emphasize their arguments. Love thought they must have bad news to be in such a hurry to pass it on, and went back to his postcards: 'Weather has been marvellous so far, and so is the wine . . .' He penned the same old clichés each time; only the names and addresses to which he was sending them were different. A waste of time and money, he thought, but then to send and receive coloured holiday postcards was a custom, and in the country, a lot of people run their lives by custom and tradition.

At lunch, Love learned from the waiter the news the bus passengers had brought. The children from the orphanage had been involved in a road accident. On their way to see the ancient castle at the top of the hill, in the centre of Giglio, and half-way round one of the ferocious bends, the driver of their bus had apparently been dazzled by sunlight reflected from another windscreen. He had momentarily lost control and his huge fifty-seater vehicle had ploughed its way over the unbanked road and down among the rocks and wild herbs and cactus plants of the mountainside.

Several children had been seriously injured; some were even believed dead. Fortunately, the priests who had arranged the outing had been in a car following the bus, and they had helped to carry some of the children to safety; the bus itself caught fire.

'I'm a doctor,' Love told the hotel manager. 'Can I help in any way?'

Eyes turned on him lugubriously, speculatively; he had immediately acquired an importance. Someone with a car offered him a lift. Ten minutes along the road, they came across the local policeman putting up a black and white crash barrier where the bus had gone over the edge. The local doctor's Fiat was parked near by.

Down the hillside, amid the wreckage of burst seats, broken glass and splintered, charred wood, it was difficult enough to assess the total damage, let alone examine the injured. A crowd had gathered to stare dumbly at the burned-out wreckage and enjoy suffering by proxy. On the other side of the road, among the loose rocks and the spiky cactus plants, someone had spread a white sheet.

Love lifted it. The dead face of a small boy aged about seven looked up at him. His lips were set in a smile. In his left hand, he still clutched a shabby toy boat, blue, with a white deck, the unwanted cast-off from some richer child.

Love felt the boy's head; the base of his skull had been splintered in the fall. He must have died instantly, actually in mid-thought, happy at the prospect of a day on a fairy-tale island, without even time for the smile to fade. Love let the sheet drop over him again, and stood up.

'Is there anything I can do?' he asked the doctor, who nodded a greeting.

'Nothing, really. But it's good of you to offer. We've got them all down to the port. Perhaps you'd come and help me there?'

'How many are dead?' asked Love, when they were in the doctor's Fiat.

'The one you've just seen, and one trapped under a seat and burned to death. It's a marvel there weren't more.'

'Are you sure there weren't?' asked Love.

'Positive.'

They were passing the hut where Love had heard the circular saw on the previous evening. Instinctively, he looked towards it; the door was chained shut with a padlock. Behind the door were four small coffins; a mile away, two dead children. The equation didn't add up; the sum still produced the wrong answer. But for how long?

'What happens now?' he asked the doctor, bringing back his thoughts to the present.

'Luckily the ferry hasn't left. We'll put all the injured aboard. And the dead, of course. The others can go on with their holiday.'

'When does the boat sail?'

'Half-past four. I've telephoned for ambulances to be waiting at the other side.'

He stopped the car outside the cafe where Love had sat on the previous evening.

A crowd ringed in the injured, who lay on makeshift beds of blankets and coats among the ropes and bollards and fish boxes. Love helped the doctor check their injuries, but apart from several with broken bones and one with concussion, the other injuries seemed relatively superficial. There was nothing he could do to help, so he hired a taxi and drove back to the Campese Hotel.

'There's been a telephone call for you, Signor,' the clerk told him as he came in. 'From London. They've been trying every five minutes. Said it was urgent.'

As he spoke, the telephone rang again. He picked up the receiver.

'It's for you,' he said to Love.

'I'll take it in my room,' said Love, and dashed up the stairs, three at a time. He picked up the bedside telephone, set his tape recorder against it, and spoke into the mouthpiece.

'Dr Love here,' he said.

'This is International Surgical Exports of London,' a girl's voice announced in his ear. 'Will you please hold the line while we put you on to Dr Smallhouse?'

Smallhouse was the cue; the name of the firm meant nothing, although it was a genuinely registered company. Love pressed the tape-recorder button and the plastic spool of tape began to spin. A Niagara of absurd, meaningless noise poured and crackled from the ebonite earpiece of the telephone. When it stopped, he switched off the recorder and spoke into the telephone again, a cover in case anyone was eavesdropping.

'I'm afraid the line is so bad, I just can't hear you at all,' he said.

'I'm so sorry,' the girl replied, impersonally. 'We'll telephone you again at four.' This told Love that the message had been relayed at four times the speed of speech.

Love rewound the spool and played it at its proper speed. MacGillivray's Scots accent came over loud and clear.

'Regarding your telephone message, which we received very plainly, Giglio is unimportant, except as a minor tourist resort. Politically, it veers to the other side. Economically, it's very poor, although tourism is growing. Historically, it's interesting.

'Two weeks ago, an Italian Air Force plane out of Rome military airport, bound for New York, came down in the sea four miles north of your island. The crew were lost and the cargo has not been recovered. It is not known what the plane was carrying, but Italian Navy divers have made strenuous efforts to raise it without success. Nothing else is known.'

The message ended and the tape spun on soundlessly. Love switched it off, smiling at MacGillivray's cautious reference to Communists as the other side; the way he spoke of them, they sounded like a spiritualist group.

He lit a Gitane and looked out of the window at the burnished, empty beach. A motor-launch rode lazily at anchor; on the after deck, under a canvas awning, two couples were finishing lunch. The launch reminded Love of the toy boat in the child's hands; it was the same colour, blue with white decking.

Four small coffins, two small bodies; and a plane at the bottom of that shining, sparkling sea; now, no doubt, with barnacles and seaweed on it, with fish swimming in and out of the broken empty windows. The equation began to make more sense. But had he time for what he had to do? More important, had he also the nerve? He decided he had both. Just, but no more. He thought of the words of his favourite author, the seventeenth-century Norwich physician, Sir Thomas Browne, 'Obstinacy in a bad cause is but constancy in a good.' He would be constant. He picked up his telephone.

'That call I've just had from London,' he told the operator. 'The line was so bad, I couldn't hear them very well. Could you get them back urgently, please? Tell the International exchange I'm a doctor. This is a matter of life and death.'

Mostly death, he thought, and lit another Gitane.

International Surgical Exports were on the line within seven minutes; Love had his message ready and played it over immediately. Then he hired the hotel taxi and drove back to the quayside.

As the taxi turned down the last hill into the port, he saw a long procession straggling ahead of him. Leading it, under sprays of yellow broom and thyme gathered by the roadside, were the four sapele coffins he had seen being made about fifteen hours earlier.

Either the doctor was wrong, and four had died in the accident; or Love was right. Either way, the thought gave him no comfort.

Four fishermen in jeans and black berets carried each coffin, a man to each corner; and behind them, in step, heads bowed, each holding a crucifix, walked the priests from Love's hotel.

Behind the priests stretched dozens of people: young men in shorts, women with babies in their arms or pushing prams, children who ran and skipped incongruously along the roadway, not fully realizing what had happened, what was happening.

Gently the coffins were lifted up the gangway and placed on the after deck, ringed with their flowers. The priests blessed the crowds, then, one by one, they climbed aboard.

Love followed them and looked back at the quayside. It was thick with watchers. Many women held handkerchiefs to their eyes. Others knelt on the stones to pray. Windows overlooking the port had their shutters closed. From some hung Italian tricolours; several doorways had bows of black crepe on their lintels.

A handful of day-trippers stood apart from the priests, talking in low voices. The shadow of other people's eternity was darkening their day; they'd be glad to be home.

Love went down to the bar and ordered a long Campari, but he felt tired, and it tasted bitter on his tongue. He walked up into the bows and hoped the breeze would blow away his mood of depression.

Within an hour, the ship was berthed alongside the quay at Porto Santo Stefano. News of the accident had somehow travelled on wings, and crowds watched the arrival in silence; every window was a frame for curious faces. Love watched them. Within minutes, he would know whether London had been able to act on his message.

What would happen to him if they hadn't, or couldn't or didn't, gave him nausea to imagine. But now there was no road back, no turning aside. He had passed that point of unreturn when he had telephoned London; now, the only way home lay ahead.

On the quay, ambulances waited, blue lights flashing. Three police officers, with oiled moustaches and newly pressed khaki dress uniforms, watched the coffins come ashore from one gangway as nurses went up another to bring off the injured.

The first two coffins were shouldered by fishermen, again four to each one, and policemen cleared a way through the crowds for them. But the priests waved aside all offers of help for the other two. Slowly, they bent down, also four to a coffin, while willing hands placed the little coffins on their shoulders. Then they straightened up and began to march.

Love caught up with the priest who had the stained fingers. They glanced at each other as he fell into step beside him, but the man showed no glimmer of recognition in his eyes. He walked on, his head downcast, left hand on his crucifix, right hand steadying the corner of the coffin on his shoulder.

Love kept in step with him. A little spark of nervousness flickered in the priest's eyes; a pulse began to tic in his neck and a thin stripe of sweat slid down his temple. Was this from the exertion of carrying the coffin - or was it the sweat of fear?

Love never really discovered.

At that moment, someone blew a whistle and the procession stopped raggedly. The three policemen who had watched them disembark were standing across the entrance to the quay; on either side of them were silver-painted bollards linked by chains.

One of the officers spoke in Italian, which Love could not understand, but at once people in the crowd began to shout back angrily.

It was now or never. Love made it now.

The priest with the nicotined fingers was watching him, running the point of his tongue over his dry lips. His face was grey. Love made a quick move towards his own left shoulder, as though to draw a gun he didn't possess from a shoulder holster he never had. The priest ducked slightly, his knees bent.

He had recognized the manoeuvre too swiftly for a man of God, and his left hand went down instinctively to the pocket slit in his cassock.

With this sudden movement his shoulder slipped from under the coffin; his colleagues struggled to hold it steady, but in vain. It crashed down on the hot, oil-stained concrete with a splintering of wood.

A cry of horror crackled through the crowd like fire in a forest. Then their horror swept, through amazement and bewilderment, to anger. For, in splintering, the fourth sapele coffin burst open to reveal not a tiny body in a shroud, but the blunt, rounded ends of gold bars in sawdust packing.

Love seized the priest as whistles blew their warning messages from across the square; the road was instantly alive with running policemen. One moment the priests were on the quay; the next, they were inside the nearest ambulance.

'Unless I'm quite mistaken,' a man behind Love said to him in English, 'you must be the English Dr Jason Love?'

'That's right.'

'Then come with me, please. I'm the local Chief of Police. Plain clothes division.'

Within minutes, Love was in the chief's office behind the houses, near the boatyard. A fan pawed the air, two iced drinks grew misty on his desk.

'Very smart work,' said the Chief of Police approvingly. 'Very smoothly done, since I understand that you are not ah - one of us - but, in fact, an English doctor on holiday here?'

'That's right,' said Love again; he could think of nothing else to say. 'On holiday.'

'Well,' said the other man, reliving the excitement in retrospect. 'We've had a most exciting forty minutes or so. Most unusual, too. First, a direct telephone call from our Embassy in London to say they'd been advised of this attempt to get the gold out.

'As soon as I saw those so-called priests, I recognized one of them. He wasn't in a monk's cell then, but a prison cell, where he'll shortly be again. Cleverly planned, though, the whole thing.

'They knew the plane that crashed was carrying gold for Fort Knox; part of our loan repayment. They knew it had been smuggled ashore by fishermen to Giglio -and they decided to try and bring it over to the mainland in two coffins.

'They took risks - dazzling the bus driver with a mirror, dressing up as priests and so on. But they got away with them.

'What tripped them up, they couldn't budget for. An English doctor on holiday!'

Other officers were coming into the room now, their faces shining with triumph; the prospect of promotion hung brightly in the air.

'Yes, you must feel very pleased with yourself, doctor,' went on the Chief of Police, pouring out more Campari. 'A reward has been offered, of course. You are thinking how you can spend it, I expect?'

He laughed at his little joke.

'No,' said Love. 'I'm not really pleased with myself. And I don't want the reward. Give it to the orphans. Let them enjoy themselves for once.'

'Well, of course ...' the officer began again, but this time Love didn't even hear him.

He was looking out of the window, over the tops of the houses and the forest of masts to the cobalt bay beyond. Yet he didn't really see any of these things; he saw a timeless happy smile on a small boy's face, a little blue boat that would never now put out to sea.

MONDAY in Portugal

Hero or heroin?

One of the more pleasant, if unexpected, results of being a country doctor, thought Love, lying back lazily in the stern of the little fishing boat, Jose Miguel was the way in which so many patients became friends. This meant that they tended to seek help from you as much on a basis of friendship as medicine - which was why he was now fishing off Praia da Luz in southern Portugal, while the morning sunshine burnished the shimmering sea with gold, instead of holding his usual surgery in Somerset.

The garage owner in Love's village there - possibly the one man in the West Country who best understood the mechanical intricacies of his Cord and sympathized with them - had come to see him a few days before with a worry on his mind. His son, on a camping holiday in Portugal organized by his school, had poisoned his foot on a broken shell.

The boy was in hospital in Lagos, and his father could not go out to bring him home. Could Love possibly fly out in his place?

This Love had done, and gladly, but the boy's temperature had risen unexpectedly on the day he arrived, and he would not be fit to fly for two or three days. So Love found himself with at least seventy-two unexpected hours to kill on a coast with a perfect climate.

From the Jose Miguel, trailing three fishing lines baited with octopus slices out behind him, he could see the whole beach and the rising land behind, dotted with white houses in the Moorish style, all arches and terracotta roofs.

Immediately to his left, a splendid white yacht lay at anchor. To his right soared the headland, from which the village took its name - the beach of light - because, at sunset, through some reflection against the face of this cliff, the whole bay glowed with pale translucent light, as though from a sunken sun beneath the sea.

The beach itself was a bone-white crescent baked by the sun, dotted with canvas bathing-tents and striped sunshade awnings. A few fishing boats were pulled up well beyond the tide, and, behind them, a rough road led past a well. A policeman (grey topi, grey uniform), stood outside the whitewashed police post, watching a handful of cars parked under the feathery trees. Love remembered how the manager of his hotel in Lagos, the nearest town of any size, had told him on the previous evening how, only a few years ago, there had been barely half a dozen cars in that part of the Algarve. Even so, the Algarve remained virtually the last outpost of Europe to resist the rash of prefabricated hutches for holidaymakers that had already ruined too many miles of coast in other countries.

A gurgle of engines cut into Love's thoughts. A speedboat with two Mercury outboards had started from behind the yacht, and was heading towards the shore, carving a wide white curve of foam through the sea.

Love looked at his watch. It was exactly eleven o'clock. He raised his binoculars and scanned the beach.

At eleven o'clock on the previous morning, he had watched a certain sequence of events, and in the absence of anything else to occupy his mind, he wanted to see whether they would repeat themselves. Oddly enough, they did.

A grey Simca 1500 stopped just past the well where old women in black waited patiently with their amphora-shaped water pitchers.

A man left the car, and climbed down the stone steps to the beach. He wore a frogman's suit of black rubber, with two horizontal red stripes across the chest, and a black helmet, the diving goggles already down over his eyes. Over his right shoulder, he carried a pair of red-tipped water skis. He waded out into the sea up to his waist, bent down, fixed on his skis, and then stood waiting for the driver of the speedboat to throw him a tow-line.

The driver throttled back his engines, and banked the boat round so that it faced the open sea. The plastic handle at the end of the line flickered through the water like a fish. The skier gripped it and bent forward slightly as he fought the immense muscular strain of a dead start. Then he soared up out of the water with a rush, like Neptune rising.

The boat towed him far into the bay and back behind the yacht, his skis weaving a dancing tapestry of foam on the lapis lazuli sea. Then there was a flurry of white, and the speedboat turned round slowly in a circle to pick him up. He had come off. His black helmet disappeared for a moment. Then it bobbed up again, tiny as a matchhead against the sea and sky. The man in the boat threw him the line. He caught the handle and balanced himself against the rope, back humped to take the strain as it tightened. The engines raced again, and Love watched with admiration the grace with which the skier rose from the water.

He thought it would be illuminating to calculate the forces acting on the man's back muscles against the static resistance of the sea. How many of his patients with slipped discs would envy him his strength! But how would one plot the co-efficient of stress, assuming that the engines developed a total of, say, one hundred horsepower, and the man weighed nearly twice as many pounds? Idly, he toyed with the problem, enjoying the mental exercise, because it didn't matter if he couldn't find the answer.

Love kept his glasses on the skier. He was heading back towards the shore. The sea would be very cold out there, he thought, even in a rubber suit. Then Love refocused the glasses more carefully, his forehead wrinkled with concentration.

Surely this skier had a slightly different stance to the man he had watched go out? His hips seemed narrower, his back slightly more sharply bent forward, his elbows held more closely to his body. But if this wasn't the same man, then what had happened to him - and who was this?

How could one skier possibly sink and another take his place? Or rather, how couldn't he?

Love lowered his glasses and glanced back towards the yacht. It blotted out a view of the horizon, both for him and for anyone on the shore, yet he had seen the skier let go of the rope, sink beneath the sea, and seconds later a head had reappeared. Anyone on the beach would have seen the same thing, but from a greater distance. Also, they would only see a man heading towards them, while he had an angled view, through glasses, which magnified the differences.

Love's experience, as a part-time agent for the overseas section of the British Intelligence Service, had sharpened an instinctive medical mistrust of anything unusual, unexpected or untoward. And surely this was all three?

He had seen several other skiers in the bay on the previous morning, but they had all begun and ended their runs from the shore, towed out and in again by a green motor-boat belonging to a family staying in the Rua da Boa Pesca, and none had come off in the water.

He watched the driver of the speedboat raise his left hand. The skier let go of the tow-line and slowly sank into the shallow water, a water-god descending. The boat turned and puttered out to its moorings. The skier slipped off his skis, waded ashore, walked up to the grey Simca. It drove off, pulling a plume of dust behind it.

'Who's that?' Love asked the fisherman, who spoke English.

'Someone on holiday, Senhor. The car belongs to Dr Esteban. He has a house beyond Espiche, about five kilometres inland. The Farm of Olives. He's generally here for a month in the summer. From Lisbon. A very rich man. The speedboat is local, Senhor.'

'And the yacht?' asked Love, nodding towards the glittering vessel.

'That arrived yesterday from Marseilles. But no one is allowed to land here. They have a case of fever aboard. It leaves tomorrow at noon.'

Love turned his glasses on the other cars; the policeman was picking his teeth with a match.

'Why the policeman on the beach?' Love asked inconsequentially.

'They check our fishing boats when we come back each morning with our catch. They see people are properly dressed for bathing. Only the young and slim may wear bikinis here, Senhor. It is a rule.'

'And a very good rule, too.'

The fisherman shrugged. It was not politic to argue with his clients.

'The fish aren't biting today,' said Love; he had suddenly lost interest in fishing. The reason why one man should go out skiing and another return in his place interested him far more.

'It is the sunshine, Senhor. We should have been here earlier in the morning.'

He pushed his blue cap up on his head, then turned the bows of the boat for home.

Love walked thoughtfully up the beach, climbed into his hired car and drove out of Luz to Espiche.

It was very hot. Old men in black wide-brimmed felt hats dozed on wooden stools in the doorways of white-washed cottages. Women grilled sardines from the morning catch on sooty braziers; thin chickens pecked hopefully in the dust.

Espiche straddled the main road to Lagos, empty now except for a mule pulling a two-wheeled cart, the driver asleep under the hood. Three women queued with water-pots at the village taps.

There was no mistaking the entrance to The Farm of Olives, some way behind the village. Blue and white ceramic tiles announced it from stone gateposts; and the black wrought-iron gates were open. Love parked his car off the road, and walked into a cool courtyard, where water tinkled in an encrusted fountain, and a mynah bird chuckled on its perch in a huge cage. The place was ablaze with geraniums, red roses, blue passion flowers. In the Algarve, with water, anything grows.

To one side stood three cars, a Facel Vega; a Mercedes 300 SL with German numbers, and a Bentley Continental from

Switzerland. Clearly, Dr Esteban must attract wealthy patients. Love wished that he could say the same.

He heard laughter, a sudden burst of Bacharach. Beneath rafters trellised with vines, two stone figures stared at him with sightless eyes. The grey Simca he had seen on the beach was parked under a straw roof. He walked on.

Half a dozen men and women in beach clothes were sitting on a terrace. As Love appeared, they all stopped talking at once, drinks half-way to their lips, surprise, wariness, almost hostility in their eyes. Love saw something else there, too: the tiny pupils, a shoulder dusted with powder, but still pocked with the pinkish punctures. So. No wonder Dr Esteban was rich; doctors who were accommodating with drugs often were.

A man in blue shorts at the far end stood up, brown, very muscular, immensely strong; his chest and shoulders matted with black hair.

'Who are you?' he asked in English.

'Please excuse me,' said Love. 'I must have come to the wrong house. I was looking for Colonel Jackson.'

If there was such a colonel, then he was lost. But there wasn't. He drew another breath.

'You have been misinformed,' said the man smoothly. 'I am Dr Esteban. There is no Colonel Jackson here.'

'I'm sorry,' said Love humbly.

Dr Esteban bowed, clapped his hands. A Portuguese servant in a white monkey jacket came out, his hands strong as the spreading roots of a tree. Surely he would not need all this strength just to shake a Bronx?

'My man will see you to the gate,' said Dr Esteban formally.

They walked in silence down the path. Love noticed, without surprise, that the manservant watched him almost out of sight, and then locked the iron gates behind him. Love drove back to his hotel. Now he had two mysteries, a skier who had disappeared and a junkie doctor. Or were they simply two parts of one question?

He went up to his bedroom, took a pocket edition of the Dialogues of Plato from his suitcase, pulled out the title page, held it under the cold tap of his wash basin. The paper turned pale blue, and three names and addresses appeared like a watermark.

They were of local people who received a small annuity, through intermediaries, from the British Intelligence Service in return for certain agreed help in emergencies. Not that this was an emergency, of course; nothing like it. But what was the point of belonging to any club unless you used its facilities?

The only one in Lagos was a Senhor Alameida Diaz in the Rua Vasco da Gama. Love shredded the page into little pieces, flushed them away down the lavatory, and drove to the Rua Vasco da Gama.

Senhor Diaz turned out to be a small round man in an alpaca suit; his office was stacked with dusty box files. Love stood in the doorway, gave the current recognition phrase, a Chinese proverb: 'The palest ink is better than the strongest memory.'

Senhor Diaz replied with the linked reply, 'As the ancients say it, so should we,' but, despite the philosophical turn of phrase, he could not conceal his surprise that after so many years of inactivity, someone should actually seek his services. He shut the door, slipped the lock and stood against it defensively, next to an oil painting of Henry the Navigator.

'At your service,' he said without enthusiasm.

Love explained about the skier, about his visit to Dr Esteban's house, about his own theories.

'Maybe you have made a mistake, Senhor?' Diaz suggested hopefully. 'It is very easy to do, with the sun in your eyes. I remember once ...'

'I didn't make a mistake,' Love interrupted him. 'They can be fatal in my profession - in our professions. Can you help me with any details of any drug addicts? Or any drug traffic at all?'

The question was so wide that Senhor Diaz could safely shake his head. He did so.

'I am honorary adviser to the District Chief of Police,' he explained. 'So I would know if there was anything of that sort. And there isn't. We're a very quiet community here, Senhor, building up our tourist trade.'

'I know all that,' said Love. 'But surely there must be something?'

Or perhaps he was mistaken after all? Then he remembered the brown, needle-pocked shoulder, the woman with the pinhead pupils to her eyes, and knew that he was not.

'There is nothing,' persisted Diaz. 'I know. I only do this work for your people because my wife, she is English. So I would also like to help you, Senhor. But I really cannot.'

Senhor Diaz sat down, began to shuffle papers on his desk and then looked up sadly as though he had dealt himself a bad hand of cards.

'Also,' he went on, 'this comes at a difficult time for me. There is a chance that I may be offered an important post in the local government - Secretary of the Commune, roughly the equivalent to a Mayor in your country.

'But my chief rival - who I think will get the job - is a nephew of Dr Esteban. So I do not wish to cross the doctor. He is very rich, very influential. I might even lose the job I have, which, although honorary, has certain perquisites. You understand my position?'

'Perfectly,' Love assured him, making a mental note to tell Colonel Douglas MacGillivray, the Deputy head of D.I.6 who selected these local agents, that he might have made a better and more aggressive choice. However, he must not give up so easily.

'Then let me ask your help in a way that cannot possibly damage your chances - and which will, if I am right, enhance them immeasurably, and put you right ahead of Dr Esteban's nephew.'

'How?' asked Senhor Diaz, suspicious but interested. He offered Love a Sintra cigarette, lit one himself, and waited, half hopefully, half defensively, lest hope was premature.

'For two days running,' said Love, 'this skier has come down on the beach at exactly eleven o'clock. If he comes down tomorrow, I want his car delayed between the doctor's house and the beach - for fifteen minutes at the most, possibly even only for ten. That's all. Naturally, I will reimburse you for any expense you may have in this connection.'

'And there is nothing else I have to do?' asked Diaz cautiously, watching Love open his wallet.

'There's just one other small thing,' admitted Love. 'I saw a policeman on duty near the beach today. Pass the word along to the police generally that there might be a little excitement there tomorrow.

'And see if you can persuade someone in authority so that if a naval coastguard cutter, or some such vessel, could be somewhere near the headland, out of sight from the beach, but in radio contact, then, if what I think will happen does happen, it will rebound to the honour and glory of that man.'

Senhor Diaz looked doubtful. What the Englishman asked for would not be easy to arrange. He wished he had not come to see him, that he had never become involved, that his wife did not have such a forceful character, and half a dozen other things besides. However ...

'If I am wrong,' said Love softly, reading most of his thoughts, 'If nothing happens at all, no one here will know that you have been involved. But I will personally speak to Colonel MacGillivray in London about your loyalty and you will receive a special bonus.

'But if I am right, Senhor Diaz - and I belicve I am - you'll annihilate all competition. So I, Dr Jason Love, will make a prophecy. The new Secretary of the Commune will be - Alameida Diaz!'

Diaz took a deep breath. After all, he had nothing to lose; well, almost nothing. And this doctor certainly made it seem safe. Also, there was just the chance, slim but undeniably there, that he could be right.

'I will arrange it, Senhor,' he said simply. 'And now, if you please, I have much other work ...'

At five minutes to eleven on the following morning a most unfortunate accident took place on the narrow, high-banked road that runs down from Espiche to Praia da Luz. A mule drawing a water-cart to the well tripped in the shafts.

The little donkey that trotted beside it in the Portuguese way, a four-legged lower gear for hills, suddenly panicked as another cart, piled high with figs, tried to pass. Somehow the wheels of both vehicles locked together. By an inexcusable and almost criminal oversight, a split-pin was missing from an axle. A wheel rolled away down the hill; the cart turned on its side, spilling two-hundredweights of green figs across the road.

Against the shouted arguments of the drivers, their attempts to right the cart and pacify their beasts, angry hooting by the driver of a grey Simca 1500, unable to pass, was unnoticed. He should learn the inestimable Portuguese virtues of patience and good manners.

At exactly eleven o'clock, Love stepped from a canvas tent on the beach wearing a frogman's suit and rubber helmet he had hired from the sports shop in his hotel, the goggles pulled down over his face. The suit was for a fatter man, but the best fit he could get. He had pulled it in more tightly with his snakeskin belt, then walked on towards the breaking waves, skis over his shoulder.

The speedboat came in, and turned to wait for him, exhausts gurgling. Love waded out into the sea. The water felt far colder, even through the rubber, than when he had last worn such equipment in Giglio on his initiation into water skiing during the previous summer. But then this was the Atlantic; there was nothing between him and America. Nothing except this yacht and a mystery.

He bent down, slipped on his skis. The man in the speedboat threw him a tow-line, not looking at him, his head bent over the wheel. Love gripped the slippery handle in one hand, waved with the other. He leaned forward slightly, took the strain, then braced his back against the harsh, jerking pull. He could ruin everything now if he fell. He didn't. His experiences in Giglio had not been in vain. But then, no experiences ever were.

Through the damp haze of spray, the blue sharpness of exhaust smoke, he saw the yacht grow larger; portholes were screwed open, a striped awning shaded the rear deck, a towel hung over a rail. When he was amidships, Love raised his right hand briefly, took a deep breath, and let the line go free.

The cold sea rushed up to meet him, closed over him. As he submerged, he kicked off his skis, opened his eyes, and struck down into the swirling bottle-green depths.

He took three more strokes through the deepening dimness of the water before he saw the darker shape of another man in a black rubber suit identical to his own. This man was on the seabed, gripping a mooring ring set in a block of cement. An oxygen cylinder was piped to his mask; he could thus park there indefinitely.

As Love approached, the man rolled over, his movements slowed by the weight of water. He unclipped the oxygen pipe, raised one hand in farewell, swam to the surface, trailing a stream of bubbles. Love seized the rusty ring, clipped the oxygen pipe, pouring out its stream of crystal bubbles, to his own mask, and breathed in thankfully. The thunder of his heart receded.

Above his head, the cigar shape of the yacht rode darkly at anchor. Two triple-bladed propellers were only feet away. He undid his belt, filled his lungs with oxygen, swam up to the starboard propeller, wound the belt round the shaft, buckling it tightly. If he was wrong in his theory, he could undo it easily; if he was right, he wouldn't need to.

Then he struck out under the hull, surfaced on the far side of the yacht, where a rope ladder hung down into the sea. As Love climbed up, the hull trembled slightly; the engines were already idling. He threw a leg over the rail, stood on the varnished deck. In the stern, under the awning, a girl lay on a scarlet towel, in a white bikini, a transistor at her elbow. Adamo was singing from hundreds of miles away: 'Vous permettez monsieur? She looked up at him lazily.

'Karl,' she said, her voice soft as honey and wine.

Love pushed his goggles up on his forehead.

'Karl won't be coming back,' he said equally softly.

'Who the hell are you?'

Her voice sounded rough as a rasp.

'Uninvited again,' said a voice that Love recognized. Dr Esteban had come out of the saloon. Still in his shorts. He didn't seem to be overdressed, this man.

'Why are you here?' he asked coldly.

'You'd better ask your friend,' said Love. He nodded towards the beach where a man in a black frogman's suit ran frantically from the grey Simca, shouting and waving his arms. The speedboat driver towing the skier saw him, too, and, puzzled, pulled back his throttles. Behind him, as the boat lost speed, the skier started to sink.

The girl picked up a pair of glasses.

'My God,' she said. 'That's Karl.'

She pressed a bell-push.

'It's a trap,' said Dr Esteban sharply. 'This man here was snooping around my house yesterday. Let's go out beyond the limit until we're sure what's happening.'

He shouted an order in German. The engine telegraph clanged. A steward came running up on deck to answer the girl's ring; he was the man Love had seen at The Farm of Olives on the previous day.

'Hold that man,' Dr Esteban told him briefly, nodding towards Love.

'An old Portuguese saying,' said Love. 'Physician, watch yourself.'

He hit Dr Esteban hard in the stomach. As Esteban doubled forward, Love brought up both fists locked together in the climactic Judo blow against the bridge of his nose. Esteban folded like a spring knife-blade.

The steward came slowly towards Love, elbows in, body thrust forward in the half-crouch of the professional. Love watched him through narrowed eyes, his muscles slack, waiting to counter the attack. The steward suddenly swooped to Love's right, kicked his leg behind Love's knee in the Osotogari movement.

Now he had declared himself, Love countered, whipped back his own right leg, broke the steward's balance by pulling his right arm across his body, and, as he fell, brought the edge of his own right hand across his throat. The steward decided to stay where he was, on the deck. Q.E.D.

The girl took a pearl-handled .32 from her beachbag.

'Now, you, whoever you are,' she began, her voice as quiet as when Love had first heard her speak. He never heard what else she meant to say for, at that moment, a siren boomed nasally across the bay. From behind the headland came a coastguard cutter. It seemed to Love to be carrying a lot of crew; Senhor Diaz had been persuasive.

The girl bit her lip, lowered the pistol.

One of her crew came up on deck, saluted her.

'The captain asks for orders, ma'am,' he said. 'That cutter's radioing us to stop.'

'Ignore them. Keep full speed ahead. Same course as we came in.'

'You're making things hard for yourself,' said Love.

The deck shuddered as the engines fed in more power; the water boiled beneath the stern with the threshing of the propellers.

The cutter could not catch them now, and once they were beyond the limit it would be too late.

Suddenly, the yacht heeled sharply to starboard, dipped in a tight circle, and turned, churning up its own furious wash. The girl fell back against the rail.

'What's the matter?' she called angrily.

The officer reappeared.

'I'm sorry, ma'am,' he said. 'Engine room reports starboard propeller's fouled. It's locked solid. We can't beat the cutter on one engine.'

The Portuguese were gaining on them now. Love could see the revolver holsters on the policemen's belts; so could the girl.

'All right,' she said. 'Stop engines. We'll see what they want. But get these two out of it first.'

She indicated the steward and Dr Esteban. The officer was still pulling them into the saloon when the cutter drew alongside.

Two police officers in grey uniform, black leather holsters unbuckled, leapt aboard. Behind them came Senhor Diaz, looking important and enjoying the way he looked. He showed no recognition of Love.

'Are you the owner of this vessel, Senhora?' asked the first police officer, in English, saluting the girl gravely.

She nodded.

'It's on charter to me, at least. Why? Our papers are in order.'

The man said nothing and Love, watching his face, suddenly realized that he must have moved too soon. The sight of the yacht leaving had set in motion a prearranged train of action, but too early; he could have no proof of anything illegal. This was a bluff that could fail. The girl realized this, too, and she smiled.

'Perhaps you gentlemen would join me in a drink?' she suggested gently.

As the officer opened his mouth to reply, a sailor climbed up from the cutter, saluted, handed him a message. He read it, put it in his tunic pocket.

'I think not, Senhora,' he said, just as gently. 'We have received a radio message from the shore. We should like some explanation from you as to why a skier from this yacht has been found carrying ten tubes of heroin strapped to his body inside his diving-suit ...'

When Love looked back later on what happened next, time had telescoped events so that it seemed that one moment the deck was dark with sailors and policemen, the air harsh with protestations of innocence, demands to see consuls, lawyers and what-all, and the next they were all packed in the office of the District Chief of Police.

The skier with the heroin was the first to break. The girl was the last link in a long chain that had brought the heroin from China, to Tanzania, then across to Angola, the Portuguese colony in Africa, up to Marseilles, finally to be distributed from the yacht at other destinations along the European coast.

Visitors from any foreign- vessel are liable to customs search if they land, but no one would land from a yacht in quarantine and no one in any seaside town would think it odd if a water skier should fall off his skis, submerge and then come in to shore. Such incidents happened every day.

So one skier waited down on the sea-bed, his suit packed with tubes of heroin, until his comrade dived beside him. Then he would surface and ski off with his load. The other man then climbed aboard the yacht on the side away from the beach, packed his supplies, and took his place under the sea for his companion to return. Altogether, a lucrative delivery service, with heroin fetching £500 an ounce.

In Portugal, Dr Esteban could be rid of fifty pounds' worth of heroin at a time; in Nice, there was a second doctor; in Biarritz, a third. But now there was only a room full of fear and recriminations, under the slow-turning blades of the ceiling fan.

'You have suffered no harm, I trust, Dr Love?' asked Senhor Diaz solicitously.

'None at all,' said Love. 'The only thing I've lost was a perfectly good snakeskin belt.'

So far as he was concerned, he thought that the matter had ended there. But a week later a small parcel marked, 'Dr Jason Love. Personal', was delivered to his surgery in Somerset.

It contained a new snakeskin belt, far better than his own. Pinned to the belt was a card: 'With the compliments of Alameida Diaz, Secretary of the Commune, Lagos, Algarve.'

For a prophet, thought Love, I'm a hell of a good doctor.

TUESDAY in Holland

The seventy-sixth face

Outside, in the chateau gardens, beyond the band and the chatter of the diners, the tireless fountains threw patriotic arms of red, white and blue - Holland's national colours - sixty feet nearer the dark of the sky.

The changing breeze blew a fine cold spray on Love's face as he sat on the terrace, and, all around, the scent of pine trees lay sweet as syrup on the soft midnight air. He felt that the scene was somehow symbolic of the whole human condition; the lights, the music, the bought gaiety on the one hand, and, on the other, the chill of inevitable and always approaching death. He shrugged off the feeling; it was surely altogether too gloomy and morbid for such a time and such a place.

This was his first visit to Holland, and the luxury of this chateau converted into a country hotel impressed him. Its barbered lawns, striped awnings, the richness of waxed Dutch furniture, all provided an unexpectedly sophisticated obverse to the anticipated trinity of tulip fields, windmills and canals.

He glanced at Angela across the white wrought-iron table. Was this evening different from the homely, wooden-clog image of the country that no doubt she had also absorbed at school? But then Max's daughter was barely nineteen, and at her age you knew everyone and everything; the only experience unknown was death, and that lay too far away to bother about.

The band changed tempo. The beat of 'Amapola', a song half forgotten, half unforgettable, and now, after so long, suddenly in fashion again, spun Love's mind back across the years to another night when he had heard it with Angela's father, a wartime surgeon with the U.S. Army Air Force in Calcutta, flying on the Hump run to Chungking. They had been in the Grand Hotel in Chowringhee, taken over as a leave centre, packed to the walls, with five or six men in a room, sleeping on the floor, even in the bathrooms.

This song completed the circle in his mind, for Angela, Love's god-daughter, was on a two-week tour of European capitals with a party from her college. And Love, on his way back to his Somerset practice from an early holiday in Antibes, had driven north to Amsterdam to meet her. The moonlight glittered on his white 812 supercharged Cord roadster parked with the Dafs and Saabs and Volvos, under the trees; like the song, it was also a beautiful anachronism of the past.

This was Angela's last evening; she was all but on her way. Love hated good-byes.

As he sat there, he recalled the parting words of Colonel Douglas MacGillivray, Deputy Head of the British Overseas Intelligence network, before he left for France.

They had been talking in the back room of the travel agency off the Edgware Road through which Love had booked his tickets (at a useful discount) but which existed primarily as a convenient cover for Intelligence activities. Constant overseas telegrams, departures and arrivals at unlikely hours, were to be expected in a travel agency, and so aroused neither comment nor interest. Love still had in his jacket pocket the slim aluminium cigarette lighter that MacGillivray had placed on the desk between them.

'One of our newest electronic gadgets, doctor,' the Colonel had announced proudly. 'Helps us to cut down on manpower - and on risks. For observe how the mechanics of spying are changing - moving into the twentieth century, if you like. Years ago, to save sending a man over the Wall, for instance, we used to tap East German underground telephone-cables. But someone talked, and that scheme was blown.

'The electronic boys thought again, and produced a scheme to transmit messages over the Wall along an infra-red beam. Then someone else discovered that this could be deflected, so we substituted the laser - a brief flash of light, and the message was finished. Received and understood. Over and out.

'These changes made us realize that we should move a bit more swiftly with the times in other ways, too. Have you ever thought, doctor, that although between this century's two key assassinations - in Sarajevo in 1914 and Dallas in 1963 - the world has seen more scientific progress than possibly over the previous five hundred years, yet the means - the old-fashioned bullet - was still the same?

'Now this side of the business is also coming up to date - and rapidly. Do you remember how, when de Gaulle visited St Hermine in Vendee Province in France not long ago, O.A.S. extremists planned to murder him from a distance?

'The killer was to be standing a hundred yards away from his victim with a tiny gadget in his pocket like the one I've got here. Nothing to link him with the killing at all.

'It was a midget transmitter that was tuned to explode by radio a bomb hidden inside an ornamental vase near the General. Luckily, someone talked, and the plan was discovered. But now all sorts of ingenious variations on the theme have been worked out. Here's one of them. You can adapt it to open your garage doors from a distance, if you want. You'd need a receiver, of course, which I can get for you, and an electric motor, but it's really quite a simple do-it-yourself operation. Or you could tune it to any VHF waveband and cause a bit of concern by cutting in on their broadcast.

'Where are you off to? France, isn't it, and then Holland? Well, we'll set it to the Dutch police's wave-length - I don't know the new French frequency. It's just been changed.'

MacGillivray turned a tiny screw-head in the base with the point of a nail file.

'There. Now push the flint down and it'll send out a constant signal on their emergency waveband until you switch it off. That should bring a policeman along in double-quick time if you break down in that old Cord of yours. So.'

'Anything happening in your line over the Channel?' Love asked dutifully, as he slipped the lighter-radio into his pocket. It was kind of old Mac to give it to him, but what possible use could it be to a doctor on holiday? Still, he felt that the gift called for some expression of interest from him.

MacGillivray shrugged evasively.

'Not much, I'm glad to say. But there's been a bit of commotion in the South of France, although that's more Interpol stuff than mine.

'Fellow got away with fifty-thousand pounds' worth of diamonds in Cannes last week. Week before that, roughly the same amount of sparklers went in Rome. Week before that, it was in Athens. Obviously, someone's been making the rounds.

'Each time, the women who'd lost the stuff were dining out. Expect their husbands will have a job charging that up to expenses . . .'

Expenses. The word was a helm that turned Love's thoughts back to the present. The bill. He should ask for it soon. As he glanced around for a waiter, the band played a fanfare, all horns, desert music, the sort of braying brass that fills the cinema as the titles of an epic go up on the screen. A compere, wearing a nightclub tan and a white dinner-jacket, held up both hands for silence.

'And now, ladies and gentlemen,' he began, first in English, then repeating each sentence in French and Dutch, 'We proudly present to you, for the last performance, the greatest illusionist in Europe, who leaves Amsterdam tonight for the United States.

'Ladies and gentlemen, I give you - Turkoman.'

A roll of drums as he gave them Turkoman. The name seemed faintly familiar. Then Love remembered; he had seen him billed during the previous week at one of the open-air clubs on the coast road between Nice and Antibes.

A thickly-built man with hair black as a raven's wing, and a flat Slavonic face, glistening under the lights, stepped through the french doors on to the terrace. A spotlight flickered from the roof and held him. Turkoman raised both hands above his head. From the left sleeve of his dinner-jacket, he pulled first one pigeon, then a second, then a third. They spread soft white feathers against the lambent sky and were gone.

A waiter hovered near Love's table, an attendant spirit on the inner edge of darkness. Love ordered two more Masquers and limes and called for the bill, the doloroso. The horns blew another chord.

'Now, a volunteer,' called Turkoman. 'You, sir? No, not you, sir. The gentleman behind you.'

A thick-necked Dutchman came forward reluctantly, tugging down the sides of his jacket. Turkoman shook his head, and then, half turning to the audience, he produced the Dutch flag from the man's pocket, a gramophone record from inside his jacket, a pack of cards from behind his right ear. Applause came up in a roar.

The Dutchman stood sweating in the light, slightly fuddled with wine; he turned to reach the safe obscurity of his table.

'Just one moment, sir,' Turkoman called after him.

'Your wallet. Your watch. And - here - your driving licence.'

The Dutchman patted his empty pockets, bemused. How the devil did the fellow do it? More clapping as Turkoman handed these belongings back to him.

'One last thing,' he said. 'A letter. You've left a letter in my hands.'

The square of envelope gleamed whitely in the spotlight. The Dutchman grabbed it thankfully and retreated to the merciful darkness.

Turkoman invited more people out to join him; a bald Frenchman wearing a blue mohair suit, an English honeymoon couple, a German woman with her hair in a tight bun.

'Wish he'd choose me,' said Angela suddenly.

'Well, stand up. He's almost bound to if he sees you. It's his job.'

'You think so?'

She pushed back her chair tentatively.

Turkoman's sharp eyes saw the movement beyond the rim of the spotlight.

'Voilá!' he cried, and waved a greeting to her. She waved back, and stood up, delighted he had seen her. 'You are American, yes?'

'Yes. From Santa Barbara.'

'Well, because you are you, and because I'm also flying to America tonight - I open in New York on Monday - here is a small present from the Old World to the New. Sweets for the fair.'

He shook her hand, and somehow a huge, circular box of chocolates materialized out of the air and was in his other hand. From Angela's sleeve he pulled a long red ribbon, wound it round and round the box, tied a big bow, and then handed the box of chocolates to her. The applause came up again, louder and louder.

Angela was half-way back to Love's table when a shout of anger came from across the terrace.

'That letter - it's gone. You've only given me back the envelope.'

Turkoman's first guest was standing up, his face red with annoyance and confusion at being made to look foolish before an audience. Also, there was something else in his eyes; fear and disbelief.

The manager emerged from the gloom, unctuously washing his hands without water, ready with his instant-appeasement kit of soft words, a look of grave concern.

'Perhaps you dropped it, sir?' he suggested. 'We all saw you receive it back.'

Heads nodded; yes, they had all seen that clearly. No doubt at all.

The Dutchman sat down, baffled, scratching his hair. Maybe it had fallen out of the envelope on the way to the men's room? Hell, if only he hadn't drunk so much. He began to search through his other pockets.

Out under the spotlight, Turkoman bowed to a last roar of applause, and then walked off the terrace. The band struck up a letkiss; couples straggled back on to the dance floor. Around the bright fountains, the night seemed darker than ever; as well it might, for the hour was late.

Angela said regretfully: 'Guess we'll have to go soon. It's certainly been a swell evening. But I wish these Dutch cooks used just a little bit more garlic'

'France spoils you for plain fare,' Love agreed. 'We'd better be moving soon. It may take an hour to reach Schiphol airport in the Cord.'

'Cord? Are you by any chance the owner of that lovely roadster parked out under the pines?'

Turkoman had come from the side of the chateau; he stood at their elbows, smiling, a glass in his hand. Close to, he appeared older than seen from a distance, but this was a hazard of all actors, the illusion that defeated all illusionists.

'The same,' Love allowed.

'Haven't seen one of those in years,' Turkoman went on musingly. 'Could I possibly cadge a ride in it to the airport - if you're taking the young lady?'

'Surely,' said Love. 'You've only done a short session here?'

'Yes. Six nights.'

'You were in France last week,' said Love, batting back the conversation. 'I saw your name on a poster.'

'Ah, yes. And before that - Italy. There is so much travel, and so much living out of suitcases in my business. To me, one city - even a whole country -looks very much like another. It's all rush and drip-dry clothes, quick-frozen meals and instant indigestion. The life of glamour is not all it seems.'

'Nothing is,' said Love.

The band started again: 'Auld Lang Syne'. But even old acquaintance would be forgot eventually; everything was.

Turkoman said, 'I'll collect my overnight bag. My main luggage has gone ahead already. Be right back with you both.'

He finished his drink, walked rapidly towards the chateau. Love signalled to the waiter. Who was the man who said he had lost a letter? The waiter whispered his identity. Yes, he was certain. He was a regular client. A five-guilder piece reflected the moon, and Love guided Angela towards the car.

Holland this week, France last, and Italy before that. A wheel began to turn in Love's mind. A name on a poster, a stay in three countries and maybe four.

Love held the box of chocolates as Angela climbed into the Cord. He slipped off the ribbon, opened the lid, offered the chocolates to her. On an impulse, he untied the bow in the ribbon. Inside a knot beneath it was a piece of paper, folded over several times until it was smaller than a postage stamp. He slipped it into his pocket.

'Quite finished?' Angela asked him. 'What's that, anyway - a lucky message?'

'We'll both know soon. It may be lucky for some. Now, here's our companion. Wait till I raise the subject. Okay?'

'Okay,' she repeated, not quite knowing what he meant.

He squeezed her hand; he wasn't all that certain himself.

Turkoman climbed in beside Angela, and shut the door. Love turned the ignition key against the Startix and the eight-cylinder Lycoming engine rumbled lazily into life.

He put his right hand into his jacket pocket, opened MacGillivray's cigarette-lighter and carefully laid it on its side, so that a firm pressure against the arm-rest on the door would push down the flint. Then he threaded the car through the park and sat back behind the wheel, watching the lights burn tunnels through the darkness.

Out on the main road, the wind combed their hair close to their heads and the air felt fresh and damp; nowhere in Holland was very far from the sea. When Love saw the signpost, Amsterdam 40 km, he turned to Turkoman.

'Tell me,' he said easily. 'What did you do with that man's letter?'

'What do you mean?' asked Turkoman, surprised.

In the green glow of the dashlights Love saw his eyes narrow. A shadow seemed to touch his face and then was gone; perhaps it was only the shadow of a tree against the moon.

'You know exactly what I mean. And you think it's still in the ribbon, but it's not. It's here.'

As he spoke, he took the paper from his pocket, and shook it open. Glittering splinters cascaded on to Angela's lap, each bright as the eyes of a woman in love.

'Diamonds,' she breathed in amazement. 'But -what the hell?'

'Give me those,' said Turkoman roughly. He grabbed the stones.

'What interests me,' said Love, not even looking at him, 'is how you've got away with it so easily up to now.'

Turkoman turned slightly in his seat. The dashlights glowed on the barrel of a .25 auto-loading pistol that had grown in his left hand, an extension of his arm.

'I don't give a damn what interests you,' he said sharply. 'Keep both hands on the wheel and slow down. I'll tell you when to stop.'

Angela looked from one man to the other, but neither looked at her.

Love shrugged as though conceding defeat. He leaned gently against the armrest of his door, felt the click of the tiny switch on the cigarette lighter. Well, he'd done his part; the rest was up to the scientists.

Ahead, the road forked, and a sign glowed luminously in their headlights. Love swung to the right down a side turning surfaced with red bricks.

'Why?' asked Turkoman suspiciously.

'Short cut.'

They fled across metal bridges, above canals, through shuttered villages, and out on the long, raised road again, between fields where tulips slept, petals folded together like children's hands in prayer.

And then, far ahead, almost when he had relinquished all hope, Love saw a faint blue light winking, and settled more easily into his seat. Two hundred yards; one hundred; fifty. The blue bulb nickered on the roof of a white Volkswagen police car.

'Looks like an accident,' Love said casually; the car had deliberately stopped side-on, half-way over the road, blocking it.

Turkoman leaned across Angela, dug the snout of the pistol against Love's stomach.

'Get through as quickly as you can,' he said urgently. 'And no tricks.'

'But I'm a doctor,' protested Love. 'Maybe I can help.'

As he spoke, he trod the brake pedal savagely into the floor and swung the wheel to the left. The huge car slewed from side to side, tyres smoking on the rough brick road.

Instinctively, Angela ducked. The unexpected movement deflected Turkoman's arm for an instant. Love flicked his left hand out across her back, and caught Turkoman's throat with the edge of his palm. He dropped the gun and sagged forward dizzily, gasping for breath. Love stopped the Cord and switched off the engine.

The only sound was the frenzied crackle of static on the police-car radio, with one call-sign being repeated and repeated. Love switched off MacGillivray's lighter. The chattering died. Policemen in blue overcoats, with strange hats and black belts, filled the darkness comfortingly.

'What's the trouble?' a lieutenant asked him, in English, leaning over the door.

'Diamonds,' said Love. 'You'll find them in his pocket. Loose.'

'Yes?'

A sergeant scooped them from Turkoman's jacket, said something to the lieutenant.

Two policemen opened the door, pulled Turkoman out, led him to a blue police van parked off the road. He did not look back.

Love lifted the box of chocolates from Angela's lap, opened it, prodded at the array of soft centres. But they only contained soft centres, and nothing else.

Hell, was he completely wrong? Then he examined the lid, ripped off the padded maroon silk, and the soft quilting underneath. Stuck to the cardboard were three squares of white sticking plaster,. each about four inches across. He lifted one. For the second time that night, diamonds glittered in the car.

'Who are you, and how is it that you are apparently able to send out a radio signal on our police wavelength?' the officer asked Love curiously, watching him.

'Later,' replied Love. 'But, before I start that, I think you'll find that these are diamonds stolen in Cannes and Rome and Athens.'

The officer took the lid and turned it over, watching the winking reflections on the faces of the stones. He was thinking ironically that not all their combined salaries, past, present and future could purchase them.

'We'll check them with their descriptions back at the station,' he said at last, with a sigh. 'In the meantime, we'll need a statement.'

'By all means. Ride with me to the airport. This young lady has a plane to catch.'

Love started the Cord, and drove back towards the main road. The night was very still; the moon had put on a halo of clouds, and even the stars were dark.

'I'm a doctor,' Love told the lieutenant. 'And thus I know that little things people say or feel or do can often be pointers to more important thoughts and deeds.

'I'd heard there had been three robberies in three different places, and I'd seen Turkoman's name on a poster in one of them. He told me he'd also been to one of the others. So two out of three pieces of a jig-saw fitted.

'When I found out from a waiter that the man Turkoman asked out to help with his act tonight was a senior partner in one of Amsterdam's biggest diamond firms, the third also dropped into place.

'I needn't tell you how these diamond men carry stones worth a fortune about with them wrapped up in a twist of paper in their pocket. Turkoman could easily remove this from the envelope - as easily as taking a diamond ring or even a necklace from a woman.

'He'd concealed the stones he'd stolen elsewhere in the chocolate-box lid, but he hadn't time to do that tonight - maybe he only robbed the diamond man on the impulse - so he tied his sparklers up in the ribbon, and then wound that round the box.

'He'd guessed he'd be searched at Schiphol airport pretty thoroughly - that diamond dealer would almost certainly tell the police or Customs what had happened. So he needed a carrier - someone whose luggage wouldn't be suspected at all. And who better than one of a party of American college girls, who was carrying back home a box of chocolates and lots of happy memories about the Zuider Zee? As soon as she reached New

York and was through the Customs, he'd get them back somehow.'

'Ah, yes. Very interesting. Full of food for thought, as you say in England. And your name and address here in Holland, please?'

'Dr Jason Love. The Amstel Hotel, Amsterdam. Here's my passport if it's necessary.'

'It won't be. If you'll drop me at the nearest police station - I'll direct you - we'll meet you at your hotel tomorrow for an official statement. I don't wish to delay you any more now, as your friend has a plane to catch.'

Love stopped the car outside a flat-roofed building; the lieutenant climbed out, saluted and went inside.

'It all sounds simple, the way you tell it,' said Angela, when they were on their way again. 'But what gave you the first real hint?'

'What I call the seventy-sixth face.'

'And what's that?'

'A cut diamond usually has seventy-five sides or faces. The seventy-sixth face belongs to its owner. This shows pride of possession, or sometimes alarm. Usually acquisitiveness, too. When I showed him these stones, I saw all three on Turkoman's face.'

'Oh.'

Then, softly: 'I wonder what you saw in mine?'

Love told her.

WEDNESDAY in Scotland

Frozen asset

Apart from being members of the human race, Colonel MacGillivray and Dr Love shared one other thing in common; both had the same desire to own land. Not, as in Love's case, simply a garden like the one he had around his house in Somerset, but acre on acre of rough country, wild as it had been when the Romans landed, where one could walk all day and not see another person, where distance melted into sky, and never a roof-line spoiled the view.

Too much of the countryside in Southern England is only one tree thick, and when the leaves fall you can see new roads and buildings and concrete lamp-posts beyond the naked branches.

Love and MacGillivray hankered after whole hillsides, where the nearest town was twenty miles away, where the bastardized English of the Civil Service - "in-filling", "existing-use-value", "betterment" and so forth - had not yet percolated, and Subtopia was an unknown word.

MacGillivray contented himself by reading every advertisement in Country Life and The Field for tantalizing properties that boasted lodges, stable-blocks ("with tack-room and hay-loft") garages ("for four cars"), streams with fishing rights on both banks, pastures, woodlands and water meadows.

This sublimation he found almost an acceptable substitute for actually owning an estate - certainly it was simpler, for he had none of its problems or its expenses. Also, he had lived long enough to know the truth in the contention that frequently the only thing sadder than not getting what you want is getting what you want. And sometimes the dream is more satisfying than reality.

Love, for his part, had looked over several landed estates in Somerset, from any one of which he could have continued to run his practice, but the dramatic rise in land values, and the increasing cost of their upkeep, had put them all beyond his reach. In fact, he had almost given up hope of ever owning many acres when a chance meeting with an Inverness visitor to Bishop's Combe had once more set the dream afire.

The visitor's brother owned 500 acres of what he described as "rough land" near Wick in the north of Scotland, that part that so resembles Canada, with its misty mountains, its fir trees and rolling empty hills and, above all, its sense of space and freedom.

Love had never been that far north before in Scotland, although he had spent several holidays in his boyhood in Coupar Angus and Carnoustie, for his mother had been Scots and proud of it. Thus he decided to explore Wick when he had a week's vacation due, which was why he was at Port Remorse, the northern-most port of the Scottish mainland, as far from his Somerset surgery as his Cord could carry him, without actually taking to the sea.

The land he had come to see had turned out to be rather more rough than he had imagined or expected. It appeared to be boggy peat, with great tracts of tufted heather, and, while he was there, entirely covered in mist and faint, driving rain. The house had no telephone, no running water, and no sanitation, apart from an outside stone privy, where two holes, cut companionably side by side in a slab of wood, held no appeal to him either hygienically or aesthetically.

Love, however, had been fortunate enough to book in at the excellent Station Hotel in Wick, and although the land was not to his liking, he enjoyed his time in this trawling town, whipped by the lash of the sea, with nothing to do at all but to savour the beauty of the ever-changing hills.

On this particular morning, he was walking slowly along the quayside, which was criss-crossed with a patchwork of rusting rails, and shrill with the greedy screams of gulls. The air felt sharp as an axe, and he was appreciating the solitude, the vast emptiness of the sky and the sea, when a patter of feet, a cry behind him, made him turn.

A boy of about sixteen, in the regulation wear, almost the uniform of his age - blue turtle-neck sweater and faded jeans - was running after him.

'Doctor!' he called. 'Please wait!'

Love waited. Maybe he was going to have three days with something to do after all?

The boy reached him; he had been running for a long way and was puffing heavily. Love noticed something else; flecks of fear in his eyes.

'The hotel told me where you were,' the boy began, between gasps for breath. 'There's been an accident. The local doctor's on his rounds in the hills, so I rang the hotel to see if they'd a doctor staying there - they often do, for the fishing, and I was lucky.'

'I see. What's happened? Where is this accident?'

'Where I work. The ice factory. My mate's got his foot mangled in the crusher. It's a matter of life and death.'

Love smiled inwardly at the cliché. Surely all human existence was a matter to be negotiated between these two extreme poles of navigation?

'Let's go,' he said briskly. He was in business again.

'It's along this way,' said the boy, and led him up a slate-paved terrace, away from the harbour. The high granite walls of empty warehouses threw back their footsteps; a cold wind followed them in from the sea.

'Who does your ice factory supply with ice?' Love asked. The description had a curiously dated ring about it. In India, such factories were common, but surely not in this cold northern port?

'The fishing boats,' the boy explained. 'There are several factories, actually. For a few years back we had one of the biggest herring fleets in all Scotland here. Now, there's hardly a herring landed from one year's end to the next. It's all flat white fish now.'

Love made sympathetic noises; everyone had their problems. And no-one really cared much about other people's.

'The market's changed,' the boy went on. 'We used to sell tons to Germany and Russia. Now they cure their own. But they still need ice to keep it fresh. That's why they call in here, though it's not like the old days.'

Even in the young, Love thought inconsequentially, the past is always better than the present; was it because that every day the future grew more impersonal and more unthinkable? Nothing was ever so good as the days long gone. The summers were always hotter, the girls of long ago were always prettier, for we all were also younger.

'We've only had two lots of overtime this year - in March and now,' the boy went on, cutting mercifully into Love's thoughts. 'An East German company's trying out a new ship, the Andrea. It's twice as big as the other trawlers, so they needed twice as much ice.'

The ice factory where the boy worked was a weather-boarded building, some way out of town. Originally, it might have been a blacksmith's shop or even a boat-builder's hut, the tarred walls blistered with the suns of forgotten summers. The days must have been hotter then ...

A man in dungarees and an oily peaked cap came out of the front door, wiping his hands on a piece of cotton waste. His face was very pale.

'Yon's the manager, Mr Ardrey,' said the boy.

Love introduced himself.

'What's happened?'

'Come into my office, doctor, and I'll tell you.'

The office was small. A faded photograph showed the harbour full of drifters in 1921. A throw-switch was stamped 'Melt'. In a corner, a coke stove wheezed asthmatically.

'It's young Maclean, doctor. He and I were on duty together a few moments ago. I turned my back for a second and heard him cry out. He'd caught his foot in the crusher. He's unconscious, but we've managed to stop the bleeding with a tourniquet round his thigh. Got two fellows holding him up meantime.'

'Let's see him,' said Love.

Ardrey led the way into the shed. A compressor thumped the minutes away, its wide belt slapping a wire guard. Thick pipes, white with frost, ran the length of the roof. The air felt cold as death; Love's breath hung suspended like fog.

'We freeze water in these zinc tanks,' explained Ardrey. 'Then we carry the ice blocks to the crusher -here.'

He opened another door. In a small chill room, half-a-dozen men supported the body of a man in his early thirties. His right leg was pushed down under a guard rail, the foot jammed against a metal drum that bristled with steel teeth, each as thick as a thumb, and now reddened with blood.

Love opened the small medical pack he carried in his overcoat pocket, broke an ampule of morphia, and injected Maclean. The tense body sagged, and his head lolled to one side as the drug poured away the pain.

'Can you move this drum so we can release his leg?' Love asked.

'Only by burning through a bracket with a welder's torch. I've sent over to the garage to borrow one. I also rang for the ambulance before I heard you were at the hotel.'

'What do you think happened?' Love asked him.

Ardrey shrugged. His eyes flicked around the shed for a second, as though seeking the answer.

'Difficult to say,' he admitted. 'Sometimes a block of ice falls in sideways instead of end on, and then it jams. The rule is to knock it straight with a pole, but if you're in a hurry, people sometimes kick it straight. Maybe Maclean did that.'

'Never on your life, Mr Ardrey,' interrupted the boy who had followed Love. 'He's my mate. He's too careful. I've worked with him since I left school, five months ago. I've never seen him do that. Not once ...'

'Have you not, now, John?' asked Ardrey. 'Still, there's no other explanation I can give. And I was the only one with him at the time, although I didn't actually see it happen.'

The welders arrived with their gear, and then the ambulance men with theirs. Love helped to carry Maclean to the ambulance, and travelled with him to the hospital.

The ambulance driver gave Love a lift back to his hotel. He was late for lunch, but there was no crowd. In fact, the- only other person in the high-ceilinged dining room was a man in the far corner, his back to the middle of the room. Something about his tweedy shoulders made Love cross over. The man turned and smiled. He was MacGillivray.

'Snap,' said Love. 'What brings you here?'

'To sample salmon like this,' said MacGillivray innocently, indicating the salmon steak on his plate.

'And you?'

Love told him.

'Mind if I join you?'

'Delighted,' said MacGillivray, as though he meant it.

Love pulled up a chair, ordered Scotch broth, a salmon steak and a large Vodka with lime juice and ice.

'Penny for your thoughts,' said MacGillivray.

'They're hardly worth that,' Love told him. 'I was just thinking about a man I saw today. An accident.'

He told MacGillivray, and the Colonel nodded as though his mind was miles away. It was a very sad story, but it didn't affect him personally.

'What are you doing this afternoon?' he asked Love suddenly.

'I'll look in to the local hospital,' said Love. 'Then maybe I'll go and see Mrs Maclean. She'll have a cripple on her hands when he comes out. She may not realize that - or just what it will mean to her. I'll try and prepare her. And you?'

'Looking at a house,' said MacGillivray briskly. 'Just got the particulars of a most promising property near Thurso. Outbuildings. Inbuildings. Usual and unusual offices. Garage block. Stables. Piggery. Engine house. The lot.'

'And the best of British luck,' said Love, raising his glass in a toast to the dream house MacGillivray never would find.

Later that afternoon, when MacGillivray had gone off in a hired car to inspect his house, Love walked back along the quayside. Boxes of fish were being weighed in the covered market, and above the corrugated roof gulls screamed with impotent greed. Beyond them lay the vast expanse of rain-washed sky, luminous, like a living watercolour.

For the second time that day, Love heard a patter of feet behind him, and turned. The boy from the ice factory was running after him. This could become a habit. Or maybe he wanted to tell him something, but didn't really know how - or what?

'How is Maclean, doctor?' he asked.

'They should have operated by now,' said Love, glancing at his watch. 'He'll be all right. He's young.'

'Ay. And he'll be a cripple. That's what they're saying, doctor.'

Love did not reply. They say, what say they, let them say. The boy waited, one hand on an iron bollard, sifting words in his mind.

'He never kicked that ice,' he said suddenly. 'No matter what the manager says. He's been very kind to me, has Maclean.'

'What do you think happened, then?'

'I don't know,' the boy admitted. 'But he'd never do a thing like that. I'm positive.'

'Where does his wife live?' asked Love. 'I'd like to meet her.'
'I'll take you.'

They walked up another steep, slate-paved terrace, with echoing walls of empty warehouses on either side, past a corner shop. A pram full of coal waited on the pavement outside a shabby front door.

'Here's the house.'

The boy knocked on the door; its painted grain had long since faded; dried, shrunken putty showed pale in the joins. A girl about twenty-five opened the door a few inches. She had been crying.

'You're not a reporter?' she asked Love.

'No. A doctor. I went with your husband to the hospital.'

'Oh, yes. They told me.'

A pause. Then: 'How is he?'

'He's doing fine, Mrs Maclean.'

'Will he ever be able to walk again, doctor?' she asked. 'Or work again?'

'I'd rather tell you inside than stand on the doorstep,' said Love.

'I'm sorry,' she said. 'I was so worried, I didn't think to ask you in.'

Mrs Maclean held open the door; Love went inside. There was no hall, only a small living room, with a fire sunk in on itself in the grate, a shabby green carpet, some chairs with cushions covering places where the springs had burst through the stuffing. Mrs Maclean closed the door behind her and stood against it, as though to stop anyone else disturbing them.

'It's wonderful what people can do with artificial joints,' Love told her, as reassuringly as he could. It was always easy to sound reassuring when you weren't involved yourself. 'He'll walk again, all right. He'll find work too, I'm sure.'

'But he'll never play football,' she burst out, tears not far away. 'He used to live for football on a Saturday afternoon. Tell me, doctor, do you think the building society will give him a mortgage for a house if he's a -cripple?'

She almost spat the last word.

'Why shouldn't they?' said Love. 'He'll have the deposit?'

'He's been saving like mad,' she said. 'We'd got our eye on a house being built on the Wick Road.'

'I'll speak to the local building society myself if it will help you,' said Love. 'Your husband will be fit for work - a different sort of work, of course.'

'Work's hard to find up here, doctor.'

'We'll do our best to help him find it.'

'There's another thing, doctor. I'm going to have a baby. Will that spoil our chances with the building society?'

'Of course not,' said Love, hoping it wouldn't.

He felt depressed. Something was wrong somewhere, some part didn't quite fit, someone wasn't telling all the truth - but what was the truth? Who could conceivably gain anything from a young workman losing his right foot?

He walked back to the hotel through the empty streets, under the harsh cries of the gulls; the boy had run an errand for Mrs Maclean. MacGillivray was in the lounge when he reached the hotel.

'You didn't miss much at Thurso,' the Colonel told him, wrinkling his face with disgust. 'The house was a ruin. Wet rot. Dry rot. No doubt even foot rot. How's your fellow? Any better?'

'I rang the hospital. He'll be all right. As right as anyone is with only one foot. But there's something odd about the whole thing.'

'Well, if there is, the insurance people will sort it out. They're very shrewd, their investigators.'

MacGillivray went back to his newspaper. Then he lowered it.

'Everyone makes mistakes sooner or later,' he said comfortingly. 'I made one this afternoon - believing the advert for that house. Your chap was just more unfortunate.'

'Maybe, yes, or maybe he was more than that. If I see a patient, and there's a lot of tension in the air, I tend.to get involved,' replied Love slowly, almost thinking aloud. 'I got involved today.'

'How?'

MacGillivray lowered his newspaper again; the scent of mystery, however distant, however faint, always roused him.

'First,' began Love, 'There's a conflict about how the accident could have happened. The manager says he probably kicked a block of ice that had stuck in the crusher, and trapped his foot. But a young fellow who's friendly with Maclean and works with him says he'd never do such a thing. He's too careful.'

'I wouldn't worry much about that,' said MacGillivray. 'Ever read two different accounts of a motor accident - by the two drivers involved? It makes you fear for history, I can tell you.'

'I know. But I saw Mrs Maclean this afternoon.'

'And?'

'And nothing much.'

'Tell me what you think happened,' MacGillivray suggested. He threw the newspaper on to a settee and sat back, eyes closed, pressing his fingers together like a school master about to hear a pupil decline his Latin verbs.

Love told him. MacGillivray listened, saying nothing, now and then nodding his head slightly, as though in agreement. When Love had finished, he sat up, pressed the button by the side of the mantelpiece, and when the waiter appeared, ordered a large unblended whisky and water and a Bacardi. They sat in silence until the man returned, and then they toasted each other gravely.

'So,' said MacGillivray at last, 'You've told me your theory. Now I'll tell you what I think happened ...'

Rain had blown in from the sea, turning the slates to polished ebony when Love walked out of Wick to the ice factory. It was eight o'clock but seemed later, for the night was dark and cold. The sea heaved like a drunkard's view of the floor. A wide wedge of light glittered across the trembling black water from the factory gate.

Love went into Ardrey's office. He was sitting at his desk, checking a batch of yellow timecards. A fire glowed in the grate. He smiled a greeting and waved Love to a chair.

'Ah, doctor' he said. 'You're just in time for a cup of tea. The boys are brewing up. How's Maclean?'

'It's not Maclean I'm worried about,' Love told him. 'It's you.'

'Me?'

The temperature dropped ten degrees. Ardrey leaned back in his old-fashioned, wooden swivel chair, hands clasped behind the back of his neck, smiling still, yet a puzzled frown on his face. Love hoped he saw a wary look in his eyes, otherwise he was making a hell of a fool of himself. Maybe he was, in any case.

'Yes, you. I think I know what you do, Mr Ardrey. What I don't know is, why you do it? Money? Power? Politics?'

Ardrey swung his chair forward. His hands dropped easily to his lap; one went into the half-open drawer of his desk.

'Me?' he repeated. 'What are you talking about? What the hell do you mean?'

His voice was rough now, rasped with annoyance. Through the thin lath wall, Love heard the slap of the pulley on the wheel, the growl and crackle of the crusher as another huge block of ice split into thousands of splinters and cubes.

'I hoped you'd satisfy my curiosity,' said Love. 'Otherwise I'll have to call the police.'

Ardrey stood up.

'You'll call no-one,' he said softly. 'No-one at all, now or at any other time, doctor - or whoever else you are.'

His hand came out of the drawer. It gripped a Smith & Wesson Centennial Airweight .38.

'Don't make life hard for yourself,' said Love easily. 'This sort of thing can shorten your life span. And it's all pointless. The place is surrounded, any way.'

He hoped he sounded convincing; but he didn't really convince himself. He half turned his head and called: 'All right, inspector!'

Ardrey glanced momentarily towards the door, a reflex action, and the revolver wavered. Before he could take aim, Love ducked and jumped to the left; Ardrey fired once, twice, but the bullets bored harmlessly into the wall beneath the clock.

Ardrey dodged through the door. Two men were heaving a milky block of ice, the size and shape of a coffin, on to a wooden trolley. Ardrey saw it too late, tried to turn and slipped on the wet floor. He fell headlong across the block, his arms and legs threshing.

'With you,' called a familiar Scottish voice. MacGillivray, who long ago had played in the forward line of St Andrew's scrum, stepped from behind the crusher and pinned Ardrey's arms to his body. The revolver clattered uselessly to the floor.

'What the devil's happening?' asked one of the men in amazement.

'Bit of rugger practice,' explained MacGillivray. 'Scotland versus the rest. But don't just stand there, man. Get on the 'phone to the police station. Tell the inspector - who'll answer - that Colonel MacGillivray's waiting. He'll know what to do.'

Love and MacGillivray carried Ardrey into his office, shut the door, locked it and then dumped him in his chair. All fight had gone out of him. His face was grey, his eyes, drained of their lustre, like the eyes of fish Love had seen on the quay outside.

'Well, what's going out tonight?' demanded MacGillivray roughly. 'It might help you now if you talk. I don't promise you anything, for I don't make deals with traitors. But at least it wouldn't make things worse for you.'

Ardrey said nothing.

'All right. If you want it the hard way,' said MacGillivray almost sadly.

Love threw over two switches above Ardrey's desk. The compressor stopped. He moved the rheostat lever marked 'Melt'. Ardrey sat watching them, knowing what they were about to do, yet lacking the will or the power to stop them.

The ice cracked like dry twigs as the infra-red heaters came on. Love opened the door of the ice store-room. The sides of the huge slabs were now almost transparent as they melted. In the fourth slab he saw a glint of silver, and smashed the block to pieces with a sledge-hammer. He picked out the aluminium cigar tube it contained, and carried it back to Ardrey's office.

MacGillivray unscrewed the end. Something rolled out; thin as a pencil, covered with heavy metal foil. Ardrey cleared his throat.

'All right,' he said sullenly, 'Since you've found it, you might as well know the lot. That was going out to the Andrea tonight.'

'It's the third one,' said MacGillivray. 'And for each of the other two you involved Maclean. Why? How?'

'Because I couldn't manage them myself - and do my job here. I had to have a second man. I knew he wanted the money. So I gave him a hundred pounds a time. He was going to buy a house.'

'And the third time, Maclean had a rush of blood to the conscience or some such thing,' said Love. 'Then he didn't want to play. Yes?'

Ardrey nodded wearily, as though he no longer cared. And maybe it was too late for caring.

'His wife was going to have a baby,' he explained. 'He wanted a son. He didn't want the boy to have a traitor for a father. That's what he said, anyway.'

'So you tried to talk him round. And maybe there was an argument and he slipped and fell into the crusher. Is that how it happened?'

Ardrey looked down. He put his head in his hands.

'Near enough,' he said.

Outside there was a rush of wheels, doors slammed and engines raced. Someone knocked heavily at the door.

MacGillivray slipped the roll into his pocket.

'In March, we lost the wiring code for Weathervane, the British and French missile-deflection mechanism' he said. 'In April, it was a new radar eye to guide planes beneath any known radar screen. What was it to be this time, Ardrey? There aren't so many secrets left.'

As he spoke, he pulled another piece of paper from his pocket, rolled it into a spill, slid this into the tube, and screwed up the end tightly.

'Now freeze that,' he told Love. 'We've got to keep faith with these people in the Andrea. They'll lead us to others who were helping them. So we'll give them their ice - and their message.'

'What is it?' Love asked curiously.

'The particulars of that horrible house I saw today. Might give their coding people a bit of fun. Certainly, it didn't give me any.'

But he was smiling, just the same, when Love opened the door to the police inspector.

THURSDAY in Spain

Five miles to the gallon

Ahead of Love, the road stretched as grey as a burnt-out rubber ribbon. On either side, ran a narrow strip of parched brown grass, and then the olive trees marched in rows to a feathery green infinity.

He sat at the wheel of his Cord, the sun warm on his shoulders. He was driving north through Spain, and apart from the occasional heavy lorry with the driver stripped to the waist behind a deep-green tinted windscreen, pasted with cut-outs of bikini-clad girls, the roads appeared deserted. The tourist season had ended and the peace of centuries was gently and gracefully slipping back over the central Spanish plain.

For the first time in his life, Love had taken what he described ruefully as his own medicine, something he had so often advised patients to take when they could afford it - 'a convalescence abroad'.

During the spring and early summer, his village in Somerset had been plagued by an epidemic of Asian 'flu, and, on top of this, an outbreak of scarlet fever that had affected nearly half the pupils of a local prep school where he was doctor.

Then, at the end of the summer term, when he had intended to take a holiday, his locum had been involved in a car accident, and so Love had to cancel his arrangements and remain on duty for most of August. Finally, when he had found a substitute, he had gone down himself with a septic throat. After he had cured this, he decided to spend a couple of weeks in Southern Spain, where the welcome always seemed as warm as the sun.

What he had prescribed for himself were days on the beach, plus plenty of sleep, and then whatever each night might offer. He always told patients that with sun, sea, sea-food and wine, one could live, if not for ever, then at least long enough to enjoy all that life could give.

In pursuit of Spanish sun, he had driven to Southampton in his Cord, then crossed to Bilbao, in the excellent Swedish-Lloyd car-ferry Patricia, and, already feeling better for the sea voyage and the quantities of duty-free drink which he had consumed (for medicinal purposes), he drove down through Spain, without anything booked in advance, without anything previously arranged.

He had ended up on the coast at Marbella, enjoying two weeks of out-of-season languor, when only a handful of people walked on the empty beaches, when the restaurants were uncrowded, and to be frank (and why not?) when their prices were lower.

Now, by easy stages, he was trundling north. He had to be in Bilbao by five on the following evening; the Patricia would sail at six, and, by Monday, he would be back on duty in his surgery. Time, he thought, not for the first time, was really an elastic measurement.

When you were bored or worried it was a nagging, dragging, interminable thing, but when, as now, he was enjoying himself, it would telescope itself so swiftly that days sped by with the speed of birds through a summer sky.

As he drove, he nicked an eye over the dials; the tank was rather more than half full of petrol, which meant about eleven gallons, enough for 130 miles. Oil pressure stood steady at 40 lbs., and, at 60 miles an hour, the engine was only loafing at 1500 revs. He stretched his arms on the wheel. In the late nineteen thirties, this car had been built for the long straight roads of North America, and for just such a warm climate, with the hood a protection from the sun at noon, and not a shelter from rain and chill winds.

He glanced in the mirror, that purely reflex action of the experienced motorist, and far in the distance behind him he saw a motor-cyclist, like a toy. He went through an S-bend, the tyres squealing on the reverse camber, while a shepherd, wrapped in the same coat of skins against the sun that he wore in autumn against the wind, shielded his eyes with his hand and watched him out of sight.

Love glanced again in the mirror. The motor-cyclist was very close now; only about one hundred yards away, and travelling fast.

Love pulled over to the right to let him pass, for he was in no hurry, and he hated someone riding too close behind him. The man came past, accelerated briefly, and then held up his right hand. His stoplights flashed red. Love slowed, and stopped. The motor-cyclist pulled his machine back up on its stand, and climbed down. He left his engine running, and the back wheel was turning slowly.

He was a policeman, in dark blue uniform, with a white martian-style of crash helmet and blue-lensed goggles which he pushed up on his forehead as he walked back slowly towards Love, pulling off his gauntlets.

What the hell, thought Love, there's no speed limit here, and even if there were, at 60 he would surely be well within it. Where the man's glasses had rested on his face, the skin was lighter; a flying stone had nicked the flesh of his right cheek, and the wind had dried a speck of blood. He looked at Love with expressionless brown eyes, neither hostile, nor friendly, simply aware.

'Inglesi?' he asked.

Love nodded.

'Habla Espagnol?'

Love shook his head.

'Then I speak English,' said the policeman. 'A little. Please to follow me. And not to overtake. Understand?'

Love nodded.

'What's wrong?' he asked.

'Later,' said the policeman, and went back to his motor-cycle.

Love followed him into the next town, past a rash of concrete factory buildings on the outskirts, then the towering new blocks of flats, thin as books on end, then the old bullring, and into the town centre.

They went up a sidestreet, into a square where cars were parked around a patch of yellow grass, ringed in by spiked railings. A few birds perched on a statue of a bull-fighter, wondering how to spend the rest of the day. The policeman stopped and beckoned Love to follow him. This time, he turned off his engine.

Love never liked leaving his car open and unattended in a strange town, but all his luggage was locked in the boot and should be safe enough. Also, he had no option, for dear as the Cord is to afficionados, even its stoutest defender must admit that to raise the hood on the Sportsman model is more than one man can do in less than fifteen minutes.

Love flicked off the hidden master-switch beneath the dashboard, and followed the policeman up stone steps, worn concave by a hundred years of boots, to the police station, wondering, like many another who had gone up those stairs before him, just what this could be about.

Several other policemen were standing in an anteroom, looking at nothing or at each other, thumbs hooked in their black leather belts. His policeman led him across the marble floor, hollow with the tread of his boots, and into a room. Here, another more senior policeman, wearing a grey uniform, with his collar open at the throat, stood behind a desk, as though he had been expecting them. And maybe he had been; no doubt the motor cyclist had a radio. The ceiling above their heads was high, and of grey stone, like the walls. A picture of General Franco looked at Love over the policeman's shoulder.

There was some dialogue in Spanish. Then Love's motor-cycle policeman shut the door and stood with his back against it.

'Your passport, please,' said the man in grey, in unaccented English.

Love passed it over, with the green insurance card and his driving licence. He could smell the sharp scent of the man's hair oil; his hair was as black and glossy as a patent-leather dancing pump.

'You are driving this white Cord car parked outside? Yes?'

It was a statement of fact rather than an enquiry.

'Yes,' admitted Love. 'Why?'

'I am sorry to have to tell a visitor in our country that we must hold you here for a few minutes.'

'As a visitor in your country, I'm sorry to hear it' Love told him. 'But why? What goes on?'

'A car of this type - which I think you will agree is a very rare make - had been reported stolen only half-an-hour ago. I must ask you to stay here until the owner of the stolen car arrives.'

'But this is ridiculous,' said Love. 'I've owned the car outside for years. I've all the papers here. Look at them. Green card. Log book. British insurance certificate. Everything.'

The man said nothing to this. He looked as though he had heard it all before, and maybe he had.

'There's a room here where you can wait,' he said, indifferent to Love's protestations.

'How long will I have to wait?'

'Until the owner arrives.'

'But I am the owner.'

'Please.'

The policeman in blue looked as pained as the policeman in grey, who nodded to him to indicate that the interview was at an end. Really, these English.

Love followed the motor-cyclist across the entrance hall and into another room. The policeman stood to one side to let him go inside, and then he shut the door. Love heard the creak of cogs in a rusty lock, and footsteps march down the corridor. Somewhere, far away, someone was whistling, and the honk of car horns filtered faintly through the thick stone walls.

The room contained a wooden bench and a window too high for him to see out of, with vertical bars across it, just in case he had any thoughts of climbing out. What a turn-up, he thought angrily. What a ridiculous bloody thing.

Then he took hold of his feelings and tried to find some hope of humour in his situation. It was lucky he wasn't in a hurry for the boat. Ah, well, there was no need to shorten his life span with useless irritations. This misunderstanding would, no doubt, right itself in time, but preferably in as little time as possible. The other Cord owner would arrive, there would be explanations, apologies given and accepted, much bowing and the shaking of many hands, and then he would be out and on his way again. Incidentally, it would be revealing to see just who did own another Cord in this part of the world.

Love sat down on the bench, lit a Gitane, and tried to translate the graffiti that other hands had scratched in the soft grey plaster on the walls. Half-an-hour later by his watch, the door opened and the policeman in grey came in.

'The owner of the Cord is here,' he announced. 'An Englishman. Like yourself.'

'Well, let's meet him and get out of here,' said Love. 'I want to see your country, not your jail.'

He followed the policeman into his office. A dapper man in a light fawn alpaca suit, with sambur skin shoes, stood by the desk, smoking a cheroot.

'You are the driver of this car?' he said to Love, without any introduction.

'I am,' agreed Love. 'And you own the Cord that has been stolen?'

'I do,' said the man. 'My name is Jones.'

Love could believe it, but only just.

'Well, you can see that mine isn't your car, can't you?' he went on.

'I can. And I'm very sorry indeed that you have been inconvenienced in this way. I do assure you that this was never my wish or intention, ah-ah...' He dredged for a name he hadn't heard.

'Dr Love,' said Love.

He felt his anger evaporate at the other's obvious embarrassment.

'That's all right,' Love said. 'These things happen. And there can't be all that number of Cord cars about here.'

'I thought mine was the only one - so did the police, or they wouldn't have stopped you.'

'Where was your car stolen from?'

'Outside my house.'

'You use it every day?' asked Love, surprised.

'No, not every day. But come and have a drink with me and I'll tell you all about it. You must be a real enthusiast to drive yours so far from home?'

'I've been called other things,' admitted Love. He turned to the policeman.

'Can I go now?' he asked, feeling like a little boy, asking his teacher whether he could leave the classroom.

'Si, senor. I also apologise for this inconvenience, but you will agree that it was extremely unlikely that two cars of this rare make would be in this area at the same time. And until I had this call, I must admit I had never heard of the Cord. I thought it was a mistake for Ford.'

'You're not the only one,' said Love. 'But I'm sure you'll not make that particular mistake again.'

'I'm positive,' said the policeman, giving Love a gold-tipped smile, because that cost nothing, and he had nothing else to give.

They shook hands and there were more smiles, but Love was very glad to feel the sun on his face again after the damp stone chill of the cell.

Jones led him to a cafe under an awning that faced the square. He had just ordered two glasses of sherry when the policeman in the grey uniform came across the road, and said something to him in Spanish. Jones looked very pleased. They shook hands, and the policeman gave him a vague salute and went back to his office.

'What was all that about?' Love asked.

'They've just found my Cord. Abandoned. About three miles from here. You know the electric gear change?'

'I do,' said Love with feeling, because this mating of solenoids with valves and a vacuum servo was one of the weakest points of the Cord design. As a result, a driver who attempted to make too hasty a change could actually find himself in the extraordinary position of engaging two gears at the same time, with possibly expensive or even disastrous results.

'From what I can gather,' Jones went on. 'A couple of young fellows passing through saw the car and simply took it for a joy ride. Then they got into some gear box trouble which made the engine overheat, and they just abandoned it. I dare say, they didn't mean any harm.'

'How long have you had it?' asked Love.

'It's not strictly mine,' Jones explained, 'Which made me all the more anxious about it. I run a little agency here from my house, you see. I live out in the sun on doctor's orders.

'With all the American servicemen in Spain, there's a modest guinea to be earned selling them vintage cars. Every so often, a contact of mine in London finds something he thinks will interest me. If I think it's a possible, I have it out here for a few weeks, and if I can sell it, I do. If not, back it goes.'

'Does he drive them out here for you?' asked Love.

Jones shook his head.

'It's just not worth his while. He has a garage business of his own in South London. This is only a sideline so far as he's concerned. He hears of old cars in the trade, you know. People who want to get rid of some old heap in a part-exchange deal. That kind of thing.

'What I do then is to put an advertisement in The Times for a student who can drive. Usually, I choose medical students, for they're a better bet than the arty type, all long hair and dirty toe-nails.

'I offer them their expenses, plus a tenner on top, if they bring the car out. They get a free trip out here, and then they hitch-hike on to wherever else they want to go. At the end of their holiday they ring me, and if the car hasn't been sold, they can drive it back. Otherwise, they hitch home under their own steam.'

'A good idea,' said Love approvingly. It was a pity no-one had made this proposition to him when he had been a student.

'Well, it gives me an interest,' said Jones. 'Better than just drinking myself to death.'

'So you didn't sell this Cord?'

'No. An American colonel was interested, or so he said. But he was posted back to the States unexpectedly, and all the business of exporting the car was just too much bother. Also, to be honest, he can probably buy one there cheaper than he could ship mine home. It's not nearly so rare over there as it is here.'

'How much are you asking for it?'

'As a matter of fact, it's not for sale now. My colleague in London has pretty well promised it to someone there. I was on the 'phone to him yesterday. I suppose the price will be around three thousand quid.'

'I know most of the Cord enthusiasts in Britain,' mused Love. 'I wonder who's buying it?'

'No idea,' said Jones. 'And so long as his money's all right, I don't care.'

'Well, let's have your colleague's number in London, and I'll give him a ring when I get home.'

Jones took out a plain card and wrote a telephone number on it; the number was one of the new kind, all figures, with no named exchange. It was impossible to say what part of London it was.

'I'll have to check that my car is all right,' said Jones. 'It should have left this morning, and it must catch the boat from Bilbao tomorrow. So, if you'll excuse me ...' His voice tailed away.

'Can I come and see the car?' Love asked him.

'Any other time I'd be delighted,' Jones told him. 'But this has been about the worst week of the year for me. I've got to go to a meeting in Salamanca this evening, and there will be nobody in my house who can show you the car - which I'm going to keep under lock and key, just in case anyone else gets any ideas about it.'

'I understand,' said Love. After all, it didn't really matter. He would, no doubt, see the car aboard the Patricia, or, if not there, he could ring the man in South London.

They stood up and shook hands.

Love watched Jones disappear. He walked with quick light steps, rather like a ballet dancer, or a boxer, Somewhere, a church bell chimed and a flock of starlings flew out of a belfry. Love glanced at his watch and decided against driving on farther that day. He did not like driving at night in an old car, in case of breakdown. If something serious happened, he could easily be marooned on an empty plain until dawn. He asked the barman to recommend him an hotel. The man told him, the Alhambra, the only hotel in town.

This turned out to be a square stone building, with ancient shutters pinned back like wooden ears against the walls, and a steep, cobbled carriageway leading to a small yard ringed round by trees. Yes, they had a room; in fact, the whole hotel seemed deserted.

His bedroom was a tall cave, dark and smelling slightly musty in the Spanish style, with a picture of some unidentified saint on the wall above an ancient wash-basin with a dripping tap. The lavatory was everything he feared it would be, and dinner was not until half-past nine, again in the Spanish style. He began to think that he should have pressed on to Burgos or Plasencia.

In the tiny bar, hung with faded bull-fight posters around the inevitable, and slightly out-of-tune TV set, on which blurred figures played in a football match that seemed to have gone on all night, he sat and drank sherry after sherry.

Another man came in, a young man with long hair, corduroy trousers, sandals and a loose jacket. He could only be English, and he was. Love nodded a greeting.

'That your Cord outside?' the young man asked him.

'It is,' Love admitted.

'The second one I've seen today, which must be some sort of record. I should have driven the first back to Bilbao today to catch the ferry, but I was hitch-hiking from Torremolinos and it took longer than I'd expected. The fellow who gave me a lift had a breakdown, so I felt I had to stay and help him.'

'Ah, so you're the student who drives for Mr Jones?'

'Yes. Dick Green.'

Love introduced himself.

'We have another thing in common apart from driving these monsters,' said Green. 'I'm in my third year, reading medicine. At Bart's.'

'My old hospital,' said Love.

'I'm glad to meet you,' Green went on, 'Because I know very little about these cars. I brought this one over a couple of weeks ago, and I had some hellish bad moments in the hills, because the brakes are so ropey. Also, you need an engineering degree to work that gearbox properly. I'm beginning to realize now why the Cord car company went bankrupt.'

'Ah, yes' said Love. He had known the reasons long ago, but in any love affair there are misunderstandings, and the frailties of the Cord were so individual, so peculiar to the breed, that this was actually one of its attractions. You liked a person (or a car) because of everything, not in spite of everything.

'Do you think that I can catch the boat if I leave here early?' asked Green. 'I don't want to push that beast too far. It's as thirsty as a camel in Kabul as it is.'

'I have every intention of being on that ferry myself,' Love assured him. 'I keep up an easy 60 most of the way, and it isn't more than 300 miles. Are you full of petrol now?'

'Yes. According to Jones.'

'Right. Well, shall we travel together?'

'I didn't like to ask that, doctor, but I'd be damn' grateful if we could. I should have given myself two days for the journey, taking it pretty easily.'

They had dinner together.

'Is this the first time you've done this?' Love asked Green.

He nodded.

'I came down here with a girl, but she's stopping on for another couple of weeks. I got the idea of driving down from another chap with whom I share digs. He did it at Easter.'

'What sort of car?'

'SS100. Two and a half litre. Nice car, but a bit hard on the old backside.'

'Did Jones sell it?'

Green shook his head.

'No. The buyer backed out apparently, so he brought it back. He wasn't put about, though. Says that often happens.'

'I'm sure it does,' said Love, remembering the infinite number of cars offered for sale that had claimed his interest at one time or another, but which he had never actually bought.

Their talk drifted into generalizations about cars, about women, about the future of medicine. And then it was time for sleep.

Love was dressed and ready by seven o'clock the following morning, which was more than the chef or the waiter were, but a porter rustled up a pot of black coffee and some rather sour bread for the two travellers.

They set off, Love going first, through streets already busy, even at that hour, with whirring mopeds and crowds of cyclists. Outside the town, the crowds fell away, and a faint mist hid the distance. Love wound up the revs, and then slid the little gear-change lever into top.

His tank was full, the oil pressure stood steady, and he had a good nine hours ahead of him. He glanced in his mirror; Green was still following, keeping station about a hundred yards behind him.

They had agreed to stop in two-and-a-half hours for a smoke, to relieve themselves, and then to decide where they would stop for lunch, but in less than two hours, Love heard a bray of Autolite horns behind him, and looked in his mirror. Green had fallen back and was coasting to a stop at the side of the road, waving one hand frantically. Love stopped and then reversed back towards him.

'What's the matter?' he asked.

'Out of petrol,' said Green, switching the ignition on and off and tapping the glass of the gauge to persuade the needle to move from empty.

'But you told me you were full?'

'I was. But this damn thing just drinks the stuff. Doesn't yours?'

Love glanced at his own petrol gauge. He had filled up before he left the town and was still slightly over half full. This meant that the car was doing about 12 miles a gallon, which was about right, without a following wind. The car had never made any pretensions to economy, but for the tank to be empty in 100 miles could surely only mean a leak.

He raised the bonnet of Green's car and sniffed around the petrol pump, and at the unions on the carburettor, but they were dry, and there was no smell of petrol. The leak could be somewhere behind the pump, or even from the tank itself. He knelt down on the road, and traced the petrol pipe, clipped to the underside of the car, until it disappeared above the tank, behind the rear wheels. There was no leak there, and no smell of petrol, and the tank itself seemed in good condition, although covered with dry mud.

The underside of the car was fairly clean. Where streaks of mud had dried, they were beige, the colour of road mud from southern England, whereas the mud that crusted the tank was redder, like Spanish earth.

He stood up.

'I've got a jerrycan in the boot, with four gallons,' he told Green. 'That'll keep you going until we reach the next pump.'

He poured in the petrol and watched the gauge register half full. This meant that either the tank was only holding eight gallons instead of twenty, or the gauge was wrong. Perhaps the tank was half full of sediment - as often happened in an old car that had been stored for a long time - or maybe a smaller, replacement tank had been fitted. Either way, he wasn't greatly interested. As the millionaire said to the inquirer who asked him how far his yacht sailed on a gallon of fuel, if he had to worry about the cost, he couldn't afford the yacht.

'These things take a hell of a lot of juice,' complained Green. 'Maybe it's the altitude, or all the lower gear work in these hills. I know my friend complained of the same trouble with the SS. He kept filling the thing up, but it was just like pouring money down a plughole. In fact, he had an even worse time. When he ran out, he had to walk six miles to the nearest garage to buy a can of petrol.'

'I know the feeling,' said Love.

They set off again, and reached Bilbao at five o'clock. They filled up at the outskirts for the tortuous drive through the rush hour traffic. Love led the way to the dock, signposted by the outline of a steamer, about nine miles on the other side of the city. They were among the last cars to reach the Patricia, but at least they were there.

Green was sharing a four berth inner cabin on D deck, while Love was up on A. They had dinner together that evening, in the Royal Ascot restaurant.

The next day, as the ship ploughed north through seas still lit by sun, a loudspeaker announcement said that passengers could go down to the car deck for a couple of hours in the middle of the day. Love liked to check the oil level of his engine after a long run, so he went below to his Cord, cleaned the windows with a chamois leather, checked the oil and the water, and then, on the impulse, had another look at the petrol tank of Green's car, which was parked behind his.

There was no leakage, and the tank seemed exactly the same size and shape as the one on his own car. Yet how could a tank so large hold so little? He knelt down, looked underneath the car, and tapped one end of the tank with his knuckles. It rang with a metallic boom. He tapped along the width of the tank. A little over a third of the way across, the sound changed, and became much deeper and heavier.

He stood up, dusted down his clothes, and went up on deck. He meant to go back to sunbathe, but on the impulse booked a call on the ship's radio telephone to a number in Chichester. This was listed as a general dealer, but what the subscriber actually dealt in, Love could never be certain, for this was also one of the outside lines MacGillivray had given him to ring in an emergency. This was hardly an emergency, but it could be interesting.

He got through quickly, gave the code name for that month, which was Ambrose, and within minutes was connected to MacGillivray. He said his piece.

'It isn't really anything to do with me,' said MacGillivray thankfully. 'But I'll pass the word on to Mason.'

This was Inspector Mason of the Special Branch. Love knew him by name and reputation.

'You've got the address where the car is going?'

'Yes' said Love. 'Well, the telephone number, at least.' He gave it to him.

'Maybe there's nothing in it at all,' suggested MacGillivray hopefully; professionals in any game were always suspicious of amateurs.

'Probably there isn't,' agreed Love, 'But I thought it was worth a call. Especially as you're paying for it.'

He came out of the telephone box and glanced at his watch. Four-thirty. They were due to dock at half past seven on the following morning, and with luck he would be through the Customs in minutes, because, being virtually last on board, he would be among the first off. Then, a three hour run and he would be back in Bishop's Combe in time for lunch.

But if he did this, he might never discover whether his theory was anything more than a theory, or whether two old cars, three months apart, a Cord and an SS100, had, in fact, run out of petrol purely by coincidence, and because their drivers knew nothing about their needs.

Green came up from the deck, carrying an armful of books.

'Where are you going, after London?' Love asked him.

'It's a bit of a bore, actually. I've got to deliver this car, and then tear across town to Paddington to catch a train to Bath. I've three weeks left of the long vac, and I'm staying with my parents.'

Bath. Forty-five miles from Bishop's Combe.

'Tell you what,' said Love, making up his mind as he spoke. 'You know how to drive a Cord, so drive mine back to Somerset. Then you can easily get a train from Taunton to Bath. Give me your papers and so on, and I'll dump your car in London. I've got to go there in any case, so we might as well switch over and save both of us a useless journey.' This was not quite true, but he decided he had to go, as he spoke.

'That would be wonderful, ' said Green, instantly. 'I've got all the papers and keys and so forth in my cabin.'

They swopped ignition keys and registration books.

'I'll write you a note to give to Mrs Hunter, my housekeeper,' Love told him. 'Then she'll serve you the lunch I hope she has prepared for me. I'll ask her husband to drive you into Taunton for your train. Meanwhile, before I forget, I'll dump my luggage in the boot of your car.'

So, at eight-thirty on the following morning, Love was travelling along the Winchester by-pass towards London. There was little traffic going that way, although quite a lot was travelling south to the ferry, mostly small family cars with suitcases lashed on the roof, under flapping plastic covers.

He glanced in his mirror to see if he was being followed, but so far as he could see no other vehicle was keeping its distance behind him.

He pulled in for petrol twice, once outside Basingstoke and then at Staines. Here he rang directory enquiries on the garage telephone and found an address for the telephone number that Jones had given him. It was a mews between Blackfriars Road and the Elephant.

He coasted into the outskirts of West London at half past eleven, cut down over the river and found the mews easily enough. One end had already been tarted up, with yellow front doors and window boxes, gay with trailing flowers and carriage lights and little notices, 'No parking: garage in constant use'. The far end still seemed the poor man's end, with a rash of used-car garages and one-man engineering businesses.

He stopped outside No. 14, with dark blue double doors, and a lock whitened by bird droppings. A baby was crying somewhere, and there was a sour smell of cabbage water. Inside one of the big doors a small door had been cut, and he tapped on this, wondering whether Mason had been able to do anything. The mews seemed deserted, except for a parked laundry van half way down, up on a jack, with a-front wheel off.

The door opened unexpectedly, and a head peered out.

'What do you want?'

'I'm delivering a Cord,' said Love.

'Oh, yes. You've got the papers?'

'Come out and I'll show you.'

If there was going to be any trouble, he would rather be in the open, with room to manoeuvre, than in a dark garage where he might fall or be trapped infinitely more easily.

The man came out. He was about thirty, with close cropped hair, a button-down shirt, a very pale face. Love handed him the log book, the green insurance card. He glanced at them, and then at the car.

'Well, that's it,' he said.

As he turned to go, another man came out of the door, head down to avoid bumping the top of the doorway. It was Mr Jones.

'Good Lord,' he said in amazement, when he saw Love. 'What brings you here? Do you want to sell your Cord, or something?'

'It isn't mine,' said Love. 'It's yours.'

Jones glanced at the number.

'So it is. Well, whatever happened to that young fellow who was going to deliver it?'

'He couldn't make it,' said Love. 'I was coming up in any case to London, and so I brought it instead. He's taken mine down to Somerset. He lives there.'

'Well, I'm damned,' said Jones. 'Thank you very much. How does this go, compared with yours?'

'Pretty fair,' said Love. 'There's only one thing. It uses twice as much petrol as mine. Why?'

'Why?' repeated Jones. 'I don't know. Just twice as thirsty, that's all.'

A man in dungarees was rolling the wheel from the laundry van down the mews towards them, patting it along with the back of his hand. Behind him walked another man, also in dungarees, spinning a wheel brace in his right hand.

Love said, 'That's not quite the answer. The tank's outwardly as big as the one on my car. It must have a false inside.'

Jones' eyes narrowed in puzzlement.

'A false inside? What do you mean? What are you getting at?'

The man rolling the tyre suddenly twirled it so that it spun like a huge top, the rubber squealing on the cobbles.

'That's what we'd like to know, too, Mr Jones,' he said cheerfully.

The other man had stopped by his side, still swinging the brace. The tyre turned, ever more slowly, and then gently toppled on its side. It bounced once, twice, and was still.

'Just who the hell are you?' asked Jones belligerently.

Before anyone could answer, his companion suddenly hunched his shoulders forward and jumped. The man with the brace threw it at him like a boomerang. It hit his left knee. He collapsed over the wheel, screaming with pain. The man jumped on him.

Jones leapt between Love and the garage door. Love jerked out his left foot and Jones fell. The man who had wheeled the tyre said, 'Good work,' and knelt on Jones as though he were performing first aid, but what he actually did was to bring up his left arm in a half Nelson behind his neck.

Everyone was breathing hard after their exertions.

'Now I think we'll take a walk,' the man kneeling on Jones told him cheerfully. 'To the station. And I mean police, not rail.'

He took out a pocket transmitter, spoke rapidly into it. A police Black Maria pulled round swiftly from the far end of the mews. Two policemen helped them to hoist the men inside.

'If you drive the Cord, doctor,' suggested the man who had carried the brace, 'I'll come with you. Then we can all have a good gander at it down at the station.'

'Let's go,' said Love. And they went.

Mason was waiting for them in the interrogation room, a tall, thick man with spiky hair that grew sharp and bristly as the spines on a porcupine's back. Love waited while police fitters unbolted the tank, then poured away the petrol and brought it to them empty in Mason's office.

Someone plugged in a portable electric saw and tapped across the tank until the empty boom gave way to something heavier. Then he started to cut.

As Love had imagined, the tank was sectioned in two: one part was for petrol and the other for something else. The something else proved to be a yellow fibre-glass packing surrounding a brown paper packet about eighteen inches long and four inches across.

Mason cut the string around the packet and unwrapped the paper. A figurine of a saint, hands pressed together across its chest, stared sightlessly up at them. He turned it over and over and looked at a number scratched under its feet. He crossed to a filing cabinet, rummaged through the blue files, and came back with a single sheet of flimsy.

'St Anthony of Padua,' he said. 'Stolen from Sienna Cathedral last year, and uninsurable because it is priceless. I know three dealers in the U.S. who'll pay a quarter of a million of any currency for this.'

'Would. Not will,' said Love.

'Ah, yes,' allowed Mason. 'A purist for the English language, I see. I wonder what else he got rid of in these old cars - each, of course, with an unusually large petrol tank. Well, we'll have to see. And as he's no other engagements, he'll have to tell us.'

The door opened and a police shorthand-writer came in, carrying a typed sheet. Mason read it without interest or surprise.

'So Mr Jones is known,' he said, as though to himself.

'He'll be even better known after this. Probably get a lot of publicity - not that he'll like this sort of publicity. But I must say, he'd hit on an almost foolproof means of getting small goods of enormous value over a frontier, without any risk to himself, or without even being involved at all.

'First of all, he persuades some student to drive an old car to a foreign country on the pretext that he's going to sell it. The car goes through the Customs, who remember it because it is so rare. Maybe they search it, or maybe they don't. It doesn't matter either way, because it's not carrying anything that is at all suspicious.

'When it goes out again after two weeks - because Jones had had bad luck and hasn't been able to sell it -the Customs don't pay much attention, for it's unlikely that a student in such a vehicle would have anything to declare, except his own youth.

'But, in those two weeks, Jones has substituted one petrol tank for another, and the one now fitted to the car contains what he wants to smuggle out of the country. A thousand to one chance that he's ever caught.'

'The odds were greater,' replied Love. 'But you can't overlook luck and chance and life itself.

'It was probably ten thousand to one that there wouldn't be two such Cord cars in that place at the same time.'

'You're right, of course,' agreed Mason, accepting Love's offer of a Gitane. 'That's why I'm not a gambler, but an honest copper. I'd only bet on certainties - if I owned the horse, the track, the judges and the bookies!'

'Check,' said Love with feeling.

As a doctor, he knew better than anyone that nothing is certain in this life, except that one day we will all be required to leave it.

FRIDAY in England

Jewels from an empire crown

It was that special hour of evening, when the world seems to pause between light and dark, and when Love liked to be alone with his thoughts, to review the past, to consider the present and contemplate the future.

The last patient had just left his surgery, and he could spare a few minutes for a Gitane before he locked away his drugs in their cupboards, closed the surgery door on another day's work and went into the house for the cold supper that his housekeeper, Mrs Hunter, had left for him in the study, and an evening with the latest 'Newsletter' of the Auburn-Cord-Duesenberg Club, which had arrived that morning from the States.

He sat down at his desk in the surgery, watching the purple dusk pour itself slowly across the lawn beneath the cedar trees that ringed it in. The dusk had been doing this for centuries, he thought, not very originally, and it would go on doing it every evening for centuries still to come, long, long after he was only a forgotten name cut on crumbling tombstone in the graveyard at the other end of the village. Not for the first time, he was filled with a sense of the futility of human effort, of the unimportance of the individual when measured against the endless mists of eternity.

A shadow, deeper than the rest outside, moved across his window, then hands cupped round a face that peered in at him hopefully. Love frowned at first, and then, recognizing the face, waved a greeting and opened the door. A dark-skinned man stood grinning at him.

'What on earth brings you here?' asked Love in surprise, as they shook hands. 'Is this a professional call - or a social event?'

'Half and half,' the man replied.

'Well, come in and let's deal on both levels. And how's my richest patient, or, rather, ex-patient?'

Love always referred to him as his richest patient, which was no more than the truth, for Tariq Khan, as the only son of an Indian ruler, a widower, who had left his princely state when India became independent in 1948, and settled in England, stood to inherit a sum that made Love's income seem like petty cash.

The old maharajah had bought one of the larger properties a few miles from Bishop's Combe, set back off the Taunton Road, and Love had been first the doctor to father and son, and, later, their friend.

Love had served in India and Burma during the war, and one of his colleagues had been the Nawab of Shahnagar,(Editor's note: For further details about the Nawab, see 'Passport to Peril') who was related by marriage to the old maharajah. He had spent many winter evenings playing chess in the maharajah's panelled study, and, after the game, there would be nostalgic recollections of a life that had gone for ever, from an India that no longer existed.

Love would hear of days when the Nawab - and the maharajah - would ride in gilded howdahs on richly caparisoned elephants, when a hundred guests would sit down to dinner in his father's palace and eat off gold plate; when he and his father had thirty-seven cars in their royal garages. Most were only used for local runs; some, like a Duesenberg SJ with an open Murphy body, and a Rolls Phantom I with gold fittings and blue tinted windows so that ladies of his court could travel in it and still remain in purdah, had barely been used at all.

They had been bought because he or his father had wanted them at the time; but that time had long since passed and the cars had spent years in their garages, polished every week, and although forty years old, virtually as new as the day they were delivered.

There were other memories, too, like the time when an impoverished Englishman had stayed as a weekend guest with the maharajah, and, finding that the taps on his bedroom washbasin were solid gold, returned, under the pretext of bringing the maharajah a present, and disappeared with them.

The maharajah, a gentle studious man, had lived quietly in Somerset, in complete contrast to his way of life in India. He suffered from angina, and any excitement or departure from his set, ordered ways, could provoke a spasm of excruciating pain.

His son, Tariq Khan, had been educated at King's School in Taunton, and had then joined a merchant bank in the City. After he had been there for a few months, his father moved from Somerset to a much smaller house, and one far easier to run, a few miles outside Canterbury. Here, the maharajah said, the air was more bracing, and also, probably more important, Tariq Khan could travel down from London at weekends very much more easily than he could make the journey westwards through the thrombosis of Friday evening traffic.

Love had passed the maharajah's old house on his rounds a few days previously, and had seen that it was still up for sale. Soon, no doubt, it would be humbled by speculators and property developers. The bulldozers would arrive: then the narrow service roads would be run in, carving up the park, and the twee maisonettes of yellow lavatory brick, with underfloor heating and fitted carpets, would spread over the once-green grass like a rash of builder's acne.

Perhaps it was this that had brought Tariq Khan back to Bishop's Combe? The rich, Love believed, could never be too rich; there were only two extremes; you either had no money at all, or what you had was insufficient.

They walked from the surgery to the house, where Love poured out a brandy for his guest - Tariq Khan was not a practising Muslim - and a Masquers for himself.

'Where are you staying?' he asked him.

'The Castle,' he said. 'Taunton.'

'Why didn't you stay here with me?'

'I'd have liked to, but I must meet a banker for dinner tonight in Taunton and so I thought it easier to stay there. He's driving over from his home in Wiveliscombe. Otherwise, I'd certainly have been your guest. Next time, I will. Actually, I came over here just now on impulse. I was lucky to find you in.'

'What caused the impulse?' asked Love.

'My father.'

He paused, and then went on: 'But without his knowing it.'

'Is he ill?'

'Well, perhaps not actually ill - no worse than he's been for years - but he's certainly not very well. He's listless, and has rather let himself go. He's taken to sleeping a lot - afternoons in bed, evenings dozing in front of the fire. What I wanted to ask you, doctor, is this. Do you think he could survive a severe shock?'

Love shrugged.

'Can anyone?' he asked. 'Depends on the shock and how severe it is. Depends on all kinds of things. Certainly, with his heart, a sudden shock should be something he would be better without. But, why? You getting married or something?'

Tariq Khan smiled.

'Not yet,' he said. 'Though even that may come. Can I speak to you in confidence about my father?'

'Of course.'

They sat down in green leather chairs on each side of the fireplace. Love poured two more drinks and waited, as he had waited for so many people to tell him their worries, secrets and fears that had become too heavy for them to carry alone any longer, either about themselves or about those close to them.

'I don't know if my father ever told you much about his position when we left India twenty odd years ago?' Tariq Khan began hesitantly. 'As you may or may not know, he, in common with other Indian princes ruling other States, was given the alternative of throwing in his lot with India or Pakistan.

'Some found themselves in an embarrassing position - like the Maharajah of Kashmir, who was Hindu in a predominantly Muslim State. He veered towards India, understandably, yet his State would obviously have preferred to be part of Pakistan, with the result that there's been nothing but trouble and strife over Kashmir's position from that day to this.

'My father's family, as Muslims, had ruled over our State from the days of Akbar the Great, in an unbroken line, but numerically his Hindu subjects outnumbered the Muslims, and so technically, at least, he should have gone over to India, although, as a Muslim, he was naturally drawn to Pakistan.

'He could see that this would lead to endless friction and he found this prospect intolerable. He thus decided to abdicate temporarily, hoping that there might be a plebiscite or some such thing which would decide the matter by popular vote.

'He went to Switzerland, which seemed a neutral place to stay, until events sorted themselves out. He imagined he'd only be there for a few weeks before he was asked back, but in fact the politicians took over, and he never was asked back, so he found himself without a future. He accepted the situation philosophically, and came to England - to live here, in Somerset.'

Tariq Khan sipped his drink.

'He brought out with him from India a number of family jewels and heirlooms. No doubt, the State Exchequer might have tried to claim them if he'd known, although he had no right to do so, and for this reason my father didn't tell him.

'Most of these jewels are locked up in the bank - Grindlays, in St James's Square - but he also kept a few in the house, in a small box inside an attaché case. He has the only key.

'Well, last week, he lent this key to me so that I could check a discussion we were having about the number of sides on one of the cut rubies. I opened the case, examined the ruby, and then discovered that a diamond necklace was missing. I didn't mention this to my father, because I was afraid that if he discovered it had gone, he might have a seizure or something. So I just locked up the case and gave him back the key.'

'What had happened to the necklace, in your opinion?'

'Obviously, it had been stolen.'

'Is it insured?'

'No. We couldn't get these jewels insured without having them valued, and this would mean that their whereabouts would be discovered, and my father was afraid of adverse publicity. Former Indian rulers are all alike.'

He smiled wryly.

'Have you told the police?'

'No. For the same reason. Publicity. I didn't want the news to come out, for I feared the effect it would have on my father. I did engage a private detective, but I didn't tell him the value of the necklace. Only that it had disappeared, and the need for discretion.'

'And?'

'And nothing. He couldn't find it. I didn't really expect him to, but I felt I had to do something, to make some effort to discover where it was.'

'Have you any idea yourself where it could be?'

'None. My father lives very quietly. He doesn't entertain much because of his health. He's had no guests, who could have lifted it, and I can see no signs of a break-in.'

'So it looks like an inside job?'

'Yes.'

'Who's he got living in the house with him now?'

'The couple who looked after him here in Somerset. They have a flat at the top of the house. Then there's a daily woman who comes in from Canterbury to clean from nine to twelve every day, and a man who does the garden and drives him whenever he wants to go out. They all seem decent enough people. I don't think that they'd do such a thing. Frankly, I don't think that they'd have the cunning to take his key and open the case, even if they wanted to.'

'Well, someone had,' Love pointed out. 'You don't have to look bent to be bent.'

He knew the couple who had followed the maharajah from Somerset; Bert Bramhall and his wife Louisa. Bert was an ordinary enough person who had grown a few tobacco plants in a corner of the maharajah's garden; occasionally, he had seen him fishing in the reservoir, or out in his car with a basket of racing pigeons on the back seat.

His wife was a shrill, jagged woman from the north of England, of that peculiarly unattractive breed who prefer bedroom slippers to shoes, and rather than remove the curlers in her hair, she would cover them with a scarf. Her mother, a living warning of how Louisa would look in another twenty years, with a soft, flabby body sagging like a huge balloon over her corsets, had moved south to Somerset with them, but stayed behind in their cottage when they went to Kent.

Love had prescribed a sedative for Louisa because she had not liked the prospect of moving so far away from her mother. He could not understand this; the farther he could be away from the old woman, the better. But then maybe the bond between mother and daughter blinded them to each other's faults; blood was not only thicker than water, it was thicker than gin.

'Do you suspect anyone?' he asked Tariq Khan.

'No-one. But I know that the necklace was in the box when we reached Kent, because I checked over all the jewels myself, with my father.'

'What would it fetch?' asked Love.

'It couldn't be offered on the open market for it's too well known. In India, I know it was valued at £100,000 twenty odd years ago. It wouldn't be less than twice that now, but it would have to be remade to be sold at all, and that would bring down its value. Say a hundred and fifty thousand.

'It might be dangerous to dispose of it in this country, so whoever has it - if they're pros - would try and sell it abroad. France, Holland, Germany.'

'So what do you want me to do?' asked Love, knowing the answer before he asked the question.

'First, I would like any advice you can give me about how I should break the news to my father. And, if possible, a prescription for some drug that might help him to bear the loss when I do tell him.'

'And then?' asked Love. 'You'd like the necklace back?'

'Obviously. But some of us would also like eternal life. To wish for is not always to have, doctor.'

'So what have you come here to suggest?'

'You've known my father for twenty years,' said Tariq Khan. 'Both professionally and as a friend. Would you come over to Kent and see him now - maybe stay with him when I break the news?'

'When have you in mind?'

'This weekend. Could you manage it?'

'I could.'

'And you will?'

'I will.'

'Wonderful. With you in the room, I can open the box and appear surprised when the necklace isn't there - as though I am finding this out for the first time.'

Love was not greatly impressed with this suggestion and said so.

'I think you should tell your father how long it's been missing. After all, he's bound to find out in the end. You can only make more complications for yourself if you don't.'

'Eventually, I will,' agreed Tariq Khan. 'But I'll choose my time. After we've broken the news to him that it's gone. I'll see how he takes that first of all.'

Thus it came about that, three days later, Love's coffin-nosed Cord found itself parked in alien surroundings, two miles off the Sturry Road outside Canterbury. It was many years since Love had seen this road; indeed, the last time he had walked its pavement was as a private from the Canterbury depot of the Buffs during the war. What few cars had passed him then went by with white-edged mudguards and round metal masks on their headlamps, for this was longer ago than he cared to remember.

The years between then and now had departed, as the Good Book said, like a scroll that is rolled together. Even the Buffs, who had worn three buttons in their caps for generations to show they were the Third of Foot, the third oldest infantry regiment in the Army, no longer remained. They had been amalgamated with another regiment. Ah, well, change and decay, etc. . . .

Partly because Love did not want to impose on the maharajah's hospitality, and partly because he thought that if he stayed elsewhere his visit would be more likely to appear casual and not planned, Love had booked in at the County Hotel in Canterbury, and then driven over to the maharajah's house.

This was a square stucco building with an old-fashioned porch where two fluted pillars supported an ornate roof over a flight of stone steps.

On one side of the door a wall stretched for twenty or thirty yards, broken by a curved archway with a wrought-iron gate that led to the rear premises. The stucco had flaked and peeled from the wall, showing old, porous bricks underneath.

Out of curiosity, Love peered through the archway. Three empty wicker pigeon baskets were piled against half-a-dozen milk bottles and two dustbins with the lids jammed on untidily. The place looked seedy and defeated; rather like an ill, old man who had given up the fight against declining standards in an alien land. Maybe it was symbolic of the maharajah's own outlook? Certainly, it seemed in sorry contrast to the beautiful house he had owned in Somerset.

Love climbed the steps and rang the bell. Its chimes drove away these depressing thoughts, not right out of his mind, but into a small back corner.

Bramhall opened the door. He wore a white alpaca jacket over dark trousers, and held a half-smoked cigarette cupped in his palm. The jacket looked none too clean. Love did not approve of such slackness and tried to keep his distaste out of his face.

'Thought I'd surprise you,' he explained. 'I had to come to Canterbury and couldn't resist calling to see the maharajah. How is he? And how's your wife keeping?'

'Much better after that medicine, doctor. Much more relaxed. In fact, so much better, she's gone on holiday ahead of me.'

'I'm very glad to hear she's so fit,' said Love. 'Too often patients complain that nothing does them any good. Well, is the maharajah in?'

'Of course, doctor. He rarely leaves the house these days. Please follow me.'

He led the way across the hall to a library that had once been magnificent. Its carved oak bookcases, with pale green alcoves and even a rare pole ladder, that folded into what appeared to be a single thick bamboo, all now appeared shabby and dusty. The touch of neglect lay everywhere.

Love was shocked by this and by the appearance of his old friend when he met him. The maharajah's eyes had sunk into his head and their pupils looked small and dull. He was sitting hunched in his chair, listlessly watching a flickering TV screen with the sound turned down.

The room felt cold, and the air was musty, as though windows were never opened. Love ran a finger along the mantelpiece; it came away grey with dust. Love could see how worried Tariq Khan must be. His father certainly seemed in a very low state of health.

They discussed the weather, the difference between Kent and Somerset air, between the cricket teams of the two counties, but the old man's thoughts were obviously a long way off.

'You know, doctor,' he said at last, speaking slowly, as though he was short of breath, and every word had to be weighed and measured, 'I think I may return to India, even if I have to go back just as a private man. This country is so cold and damp, and it's almost impossible to get anyone to look after me.'

'What about the Bramhalls?' asked Love.

'Well, they're all right in their way. But she's grown lazy since we've moved - they were better in Somerset, you know. And somehow I don't seem able to find anyone else. This last week or so I haven't been able to concentrate much, for some reason. I suppose it's the weather or my heart, or just my age. I don't know.

'Anyhow, the Bramhalls go on holiday at the weekend - she's already gone - and it'll be very lonely here on my own, with only a daily woman coming in. I haven't made up my mind yet about going, but I'm thinking about it very seriously.'

His voice tailed away as though he lacked the strength to say more.

Love stayed to dinner, a plate of cold pie eked out with a tin of tongue. The old man drank a glass of warm milk that Bramhall brought him, and perked up for a time. Then he seemed to sag in his chair as though the effort of conversation was too much to be borne. He kept yawning and glancing surreptitiously at his watch as though anxious to go to bed. At half-past-nine, Love said goodnight and Bramhall showed him to his car.

'The maharajah doesn't look too well,' said Love. 'Is he seeing a doctor here?'

Bramhall shook his head.

'No, sir. He tells me it's the climate. I think he's a bit worried because I'm going on holiday on Sunday. I'm joining my wife in France. There's a pigeon race I want my birds to take part in on Sunday. A cross-Channel race. It should be quite something. My wife's over there to see fair play. Tell me, doctor, do you know anything about birds?'

'Not feathered ones.'

'Ah. Well, many pigeons can fly home from up to 70 miles away. We used them in the war, you know. That's when I first became interested. We had them in planes sometimes, to send back details of their last fix if they had engine trouble or were shot down. I was in a unit that intercepted homing pigeons and decoded their messages.'

'How do you organize a race of this kind?'

Love didn't really want to know, but he felt he should show some interest.

'It depends on the size and importance of the race, really. I belong to a fanciers' club, and when any member wants to race, he just rings round until he finds someone who's willing to take him on. We swop baskets of birds, usually by train, and then we check our times on the 'phone, and open both baskets at exactly the same moment.

'In this case, I'm being a bit more ambitious. I'm trying for the Continent. Someone in Northern France has contacted me, and we're each exchanging half-a-dozen. That's where my wife's gone. She's just as keen.'

'Really?' said Love, trying to sound as though this information interested him. He could never understand the attraction of other people's hobbies, but then he knew that many also found it impossible to believe he actually enjoyed crawling under his Cord in a freezing wind to make some adjustment.

And, maybe, if he was absolutely honest, he'd admit that he didn't - but he did enjoy the result of that adjustment when the car ran as smoothly as a tap. Probably many other hobbies had the same perverse attractions; the end was worth uncomfortable means required to reach it.

Love climbed into his car.

'How do you send your half-dozen birds to France?' he asked, turning the key against the Startix.

'Over in a basket by ferry to Calais. He sends his to Dover, and then they're put on the train to me here. I pick them up at Canterbury station, and give them food and water. My wife will 'phone me on Sunday morning, and then, at exactly the same moment, we'll both open our baskets and - they're off!'

'When do they arrive?'

'Tomorrow afternoon. They'll get one night's sleep here. We plan to release them at seven on Sunday.'

'Why so early?'

'Because the air's clearer then. And there are fewer private planes about and fewer birds that might confuse them or put them off course. Swallows, starlings and so on.'

'Fascinating,' said Love as sincerely as he could, and drove back to his hotel.

He parked and went up to his room. There, he opened a bottle marked "Poison: not to be taken internally', which he kept on his bedside table. In this, he carried Masquers vodka, to avoid corkage, a custom that always irritated him. He poured half into his tooth glass and added lime from a bottle marked "Urine sample: with care', which contained fresh lime juice. It didn't taste as sharp as it would with ice, but it was still pretty good.

He picked up the telephone and asked the operator for his own number in Bishop's Combe. When his housekeeper, Mrs Hunter, answered, he asked her to look out a file on a patient and to read out to him what it contained. As she spoke, he made a few notes on the back of an envelope. Then he sat down on the bed, opened his diary, and looked up MacGillivray's secret night number.

Something about the maharajah's appearance and attitude worried him. The theft of an uninsured necklace, the imminent departure of a servant grown slack and indolent, and the unaccountable lethargy of a man who, only months before, despite his heart condition, had been alert, all caused Love a deep unease.

He crossed the room and stood looking out of the window at the street beneath, wondering what Chaucer's pilgrims would think of the city now. He turned over the day's happenings in his mind, and then he made his decision. He picked up the telephone, and asked the operator for the number.

It rang a few times and a sleepy voice asked, 'Yes?' in his ear. Love explained who he was and where he was. Sleepiness left MacGillivray's Scottish brogue.

'That's not quite my field,' he said. 'As you know, my section doesn't operate in this country. Only overseas. But I'll get Inspector Mason of the Special Branch to ring you back. He's the man you want - if you want anyone.'

Mason was through in an hour, his voice laconic and flat. Love wondered whether he had also been asleep, or whether he was on duty.

'You haven't given me much time,' Mason complained.

'I know that,' said Love. 'But you've got all there is.'

'O.K.,' said Mason. 'See you Sunday, then. Now, if you agree, this is what I suggest we do ...'

Love replaced the telephone, set his alarm watch to eight o'clock, undressed and went to bed. Much of the next day, he spent walking around the largely rebuilt city. He visited the cathedral, and then drove east to the coast at Tankerton, where he had spent so many summer holidays when he was a boy. The beach, covered with smooth stones the size of eggs, the rows of changing huts, the stretch of grass and shelters on the cliff top, all seemed the same.

It was cheering to have visible assurance that, despite so much strident evidence to the contrary, some things didn't appear to change. The great danger of making any sentimental journey was not that everything had changed so drastically, but that you had also changed yourself - without realizing it.

At seven on the following morning, with the boom of cathedral bells echoing in his ears, he drove out on the Sturry Road, empty now as it had been when he had walked there, years ago. A mile past the barracks, a builder's lorry had pulled off up into the bank at one side. He stopped behind this and climbed up into the cab.

Inspector Mason introduced himself. He wore uniform under a raincoat and Love could hear the scuff of heavy boots on the floor behind them, and now and then a muffled voice from the back of the truck.

'I've got half-a-dozen men with me,' explained Mason. 'There may be trouble, though from what you tell me I don't think so.'

A walkie-talkie set crackled on the seat beside him. Mason picked it up and pressed the switch. A voice said, as though reporting some item of interest, 'We have heard from our friends that the woman you have described is at the house. There's another woman there, too. Older, and English. The householder is also there. He is known to us. They have also checked he released his pigeons about half-an-hour ago. Over to you.'

'Over and out,' said Mason, and put down the set.

In the distance, coming towards them, a car grew larger on the empty road. It was travelling slowly. Mason handed a pair of Zeiss binoculars to Love. He focused them and saw Bramhall at the wheel, lighting a cigarette. A transparent plastic cover flapped like a broken wing over two suitcases on the roof.

'That's the man,' said Love, handing back the glasses.

Mason tapped on the wall behind him. A uniformed constable jumped down from the back, walked out slowly into the road, and held up his hand. Bramhall slowed and then stopped.

'What's wrong?' he asked, winding down his window.

Love put up his handkerchief to his face as though to blow his nose, for he was not anxious to be recognised.

'Nothing,' said the constable. 'Only routine check.'

'What for?'

'A matter of a hundred and fifty thousand pounds,' said Mason conversationally, opening the door of the cab, and jumping down beside him. 'A necklace.'

'A hundred and fifty thousand pounds,' repeated Bramhall in astonishment. 'Are you crazy?'

His eyes flicked towards Love, and as he recognized him he jammed down his foot on the accelerator.

The little car leaped forward. It only jumped for ten feet, for while Bramhall had been talking, another policeman had come round behind the car from the far side of the lorry. He carried a nylon tow-rope with a hook at each end. He slipped one of these round the car bumper; the other was already secured to the lorry. Bramhall's rear tyres spun uselessly on the tarmac, smoking with their speed, while Mason shook his head in admonishment.

'That was naughty,' he said sadly, and leaned over Bramhall into the car. He turned off the ignition and took away the key.

'You might as well come quietly,' he said, and Bramhall did just that.

Mason picked up his walkie-talkie.

'Get on to France,' he told his headquarters. 'The man at this end tried to make a bolt for it. Keep tabs on the woman. And lock up those birds. They've got to be searched!'

Later, in the County Hotel, Mason relaxed sufficiently to have a treble whisky.

'Neat bit of work on your part,' he told Love approvingly.

'Simple rather than neat,' replied Love, and really it had been.

The first clue had come when he had seen the maharajah's narrowed pupils, one of the tell-tale symptoms of morphia which he had prescribed for Mrs Bramhall.

He had telephoned Mrs Hunter to check on the treatment he had given her to calm her down. At first, he had prescribed Tuinal capsules, and then, when she said this wasn't helping her sufficiently, he had given her morphia. Joined, like links in a chain, with Bramhall's pigeon race, his sudden slackness, and the fact that his wife had already crossed the Channel, this fact became important.

Mason, for his part, had first checked the Bramhalls with 'Traces', the enormous and complex filing system and central register in MacGillivray's department, that lists every fine, complaint or criminal activity proved against every member of the public. Neither was known, but Louisa's mother had worked in a Liverpool jewellery shop for two years. And while there, the shop had suffered from several thefts.

The trail was growing warmer now: facts fitted like mosaic chips to build a convincing picture of a clever crime.

Mason then contacted a retired police sergeant who lived at Herne Bay a few miles from Canterbury and occasionally raced pigeons he kept in the loft of his garage. This sergeant had been pleased to take his pigeons to Dover in their baskets, and through his contacts with the railway police, had located the French pigeons and simply exchanged them with his own, six for six.

When Bramhall had collected these baskets, he fed the birds, and carefully secured each jewel of the necklace around their legs with Sellotape. Then, at the pre-arranged time, he released them. They did not fly to France, where his wife was waiting to intercept them, but simply down the road to Herne Bay, and back into their home above the garage of the old police sergeant.

It was, Love had to agree, an extremely ingenious scheme for removing a valuable necklace, first from its owner, and then from the country without the tedious, and possibly hazardous, business of smuggling it out personally.

Bramhall had seen the maharajah's necklace one day and told his mother-in-law how valuable it must be. From his description, she was convinced that it was indeed of very great value - but how to steal it without the old man knowing? And, having stolen the necklace, how to take it out of the country, when you might be under suspicion of the theft?

The three of them had worked at the problem, and came up with a two-tier plan. First, Mrs Bramhall went to her local doctor, and, explaining how upset she was at the prospect of leaving her mother, she asked for a sedative.

He had prescribed Tuinal, but within a week she was back, complaining that the tablets had no effect; and so he had given her a prescription for morphia.

Mrs Bramhall now had sufficient drugs to make an ailing old man fall asleep after lunch, and, having induced this habit over a few weeks, her husband removed the key from his chain, opened the case and then replaced the key without the maharajah waking.

The second stage was to arrange for a pigeon race with a fancier in France. Mrs Bramhall was to explain to him that they were trying out old wartime techniques of using birds as carriers. The jewels were wrapped in Sellotape and she would simply say they were makeweight stones - which, of course, they were.

Yes, it was all very clever, and it could have, worked; in fact, it should have worked, and no doubt would have done, had not

Jason Love been Mrs Bramhall's doctor - and the maharajah's friend. For when he visited him and realized from his pinhead pupils that morphia was being administered to the old man - although he had not seen a doctor - he asked his housekeeper to look up Mrs Bramhall's file, and let him know what he had prescribed for her.

Thus, what had been a patiently conceived operation to steal and export a valuable necklace, became instead the means of bringing the Bramhalls before the Canterbury magistrates at the next Quarter Sessions -and gave a retired police sergeant in Herne Bay the chance of acquiring at a knock-down price, six fine racing pigeons which he could not otherwise have afforded.

SATURDAY in the Surgery

An echo from the past

The man was small and slight, with a sallow face, as though he had spent too long in a hot climate, and now, in England, he missed the heat.

He wore a ready-made suit of a rather old-fashioned cut, and a cheap drip-dry shirt; the collar had crimped along the edge, and the knot of his tie was pulled so tight that the cloth had frayed.

He sidled cautiously around the door of the surgery, as though he had no right to be there and, if discovered, might be asked to leave. He nodded to Love, and then sat down in the patient's chair. Love did not recognize him, but then there was no reason why he should; he had never seen him before.

Also, Love was tired; he had been on the go since half past three that morning, when he had been called out to deliver a baby girl in a cottage on the edge of the Quantocks. He hoped he could be rid of the man quickly. He was not in the mood to listen to a long, involved account of vague pains moving through his body, of headaches and other unrelated symptoms. He wasn't even on duty, for this was Saturday evening, and he was in the surgery looking out some drug pamphlets that he had filed away some weeks before.

He raised his eyebrows enquiringly. The man washed his hands without water, wringing the fingers until the joints cracked like tiny dry twigs.

'I'm down here on holiday, doctor,' he said diffidently. 'The caravan site. Outside Minehead.'

He paused. It was some years since Love had heard that singsong voice, that almost Welsh intonation of the Eurasian. This would explain the man's colour, he thought. And also his unctuousness, his sad lack of self-confidence.

'There's no surgery tonight, you know,' Love pointed out.

'Oh, I'm sorry. I didn't know.'

The man still sat there, staring at Love in a dim and despairing sort of way.

'What's the trouble, now you're here?'

There must be some trouble; no stranger would come out from Minehead, nearly fifteen miles away, on a February Saturday evening unless he was in trouble of some sort.

'My stomach. I can't keep any food down. I've tried bicarbonate of soda. All sorts of things. And I can't go on like this any longer. Can you get me into hospital - where I can be looked after?'

His voice grew shrill with the question.

'You've no-one to look after you, then?' Love asked him. It wasn't often that a patient said he wanted to go into hospital at his initial visit.

The man shook his head.

'My wife's gone off,' he said simply. 'We had a daughter, but she took her, too. I haven't seen either of them for years.'

'I see.'

Love had not expected these revelations so quickly. 'But why come and see me now? It's only by chance I'm here at all.'

'I had to come, doctor. I had to.'

'Why? Is the pain so bad?'

'Yes. The pain is bad, very bad.'

'Do you do your own cooking? Is that what's given you indigestion?'

'No, doctor. It's not that. I'm not a bad cook at all. Not just fish fingers and frozen peas and tins of beans, either.'

He smiled, a thin rather sad smile.

'And how long have you had this inability to keep down your food?'

'Off and on for twenty years,' the man said.

'Twenty years? So, what made you come to see me now?' asked Love. 'Have you had treatment for this before? Or has it suddenly grown so bad you felt you had to consult a doctor on this particular Saturday night?'

'Oh, I've been to doctors off and on for years. They've given me the usual stuff. Bismuth. Milk of magnesia. That type of thing. It helps a bit, but the trouble always comes back.'

'Well, let's have a look at you,' said Love, without enthusiasm. 'First, what's your name?'

He picked up his pen to make out the patient's card.

'Windsor,' said the man. 'John Windsor.'

'Your address?'

He paused.

'Just say the caravan site, doctor.'

'You have no home address?'

The man swallowed.

'I would rather not give it unless I have to.'

People had their reasons. His could be that he was shacked up in a caravan with some woman.

'As you wish,' said Love easily. 'Now, what made you come and see me out here instead of going to a doctor in Minehead?'

'I'll be honest with you, doctor,' said Windsor, using a phrase that Love knew from experience inevitably preceded a lie, or if not a lie direct, then at least a little careful manipulation of the truth.

'I went to the first one. He hadn't a surgery. The second was on holiday, so I looked at a list outside a chemist's shop and saw your name.'

'Hm,' said Love, not at all convinced. But then did any patient ever tell all the truth, even about small and unimportant things like this? Man was, by nature, a devious animal.

'Now, a few details, Mr Windsor,' he said briskly.

He noted them down as the man spoke; his age, forty-eight. Occupation, service engineer in a TV shop in Ealing. Place of birth, Penang.

'A long time since I was there,' said Love, trying to find something they could share, some brief meeting place for their minds. He remembered, over an uncomfortably wide chasm of years, the rickshaws in the streets, the naval patrol in white duck rounding up stragglers from the ships, the taxi-dancers in The Happy World, the wonderful Chinese food.

He had spent a few weeks in Penang in the army just after the war, waiting to be repatriated and demobilized. How long ago all that seemed now! All those who were young then were now in middle age; the girls of those days, the WAAFs and the WRNS in their starched khaki drill, were all matrons. Why was everything in the past golden in retrospect and everything in the future golden with promise, while only the present seemed drab?

'Been back recently?' Love asked.

Windsor shook his head.

'I left there just after the Japs came in forty-two. I've no wish to go back. I wouldn't know anyone there now. Or even the place itself. Been a lot of building and so on, doctor. And other changes. Like over here.'

He was holding his hands together while he spoke so that his flesh gleamed white as bone on his knuckles. Love said nothing. He had heard the stories of the great wartime betrayal in Penang, when only Europeans had been evacuated, and the Asians and Eurasians had been left to whatever the Japanese could offer; mostly, imprisonment; frequently, torture; sometimes, death.

Looking at Windsor, Love wondered how he had fared. He brought his mind back to the present, put down his pen, told Windsor to remove his jacket and take off his shirt, and gave him all the routine tests; heart, blood-pressure, tongue, eyeballs, breathing. He might as well do the job properly, even if he wasn't supposed to be on duty.

There seemed nothing very much the matter with Windsor. Was indigestion the real reason for his visit, or was this only an excuse, a cover for something else? His heartbeat was slightly fast. His skin felt dry and taut. He could be afraid of something, or somebody. And fear could also produce the pains of nervous dyspepsia.

'I'll give you some medicine for your stomach now,' Love told him. 'And a prescription for something else that you can get from the chemist on Monday.'

He went into the anteroom, unlocked the glass-fronted drug cupboard, took out some Librium capsules to try and soothe the man's nerves, and a bottle of Aludrox for his stomach.

'Take these now,' he said, holding out the capsules in his palm. 'And then two teaspoonfuls of this white stuff. Then come and see me in two days' time. If you've had this trouble for twenty years, it may take a bit of getting rid of.'

'That's what I thought,' said Windsor quickly. 'Wouldn't it be easier to treat in hospital? Can't you fit me in somewhere? It's a rest I want. To get away from things.'

'What things?' Love asked him bluntly.

Windsor's eyes held his for a moment, and he saw fear and an immeasurable depth of loneliness looking at him.

'Mr Windsor,' Love went on, more gently. 'I don't think that you've been entirely frank with me. I can only help you if you'll let me help you. I think that you're afraid of something, and this fear brings on your indigestion.

'To try and cure the result without finding the cause and getting rid of that - if we can - is like attempting to treat a bruise when a bone is broken beneath the flesh.

'What are you afraid of?'

Windsor swallowed. His forehead shone under a sudden patina of sweat; his tongue moistened dry lips.

'I'm afraid for my life, doctor,' he said simply.

'Why?'

'A man we both know - called MacGillivray -said that if I could get to you, you'd help me. So I came.'

Love opened his mouth to reply, and at that moment, the intercom buzzed on his desk. Mrs Hunter's voice spoke.

'A call from London for you, doctor. He won't give his name, but he says, it's important.'

'Put him on,' said Love, and picked up the telephone.

'Excuse me,' he said to Windsor and swivelled slightly away from him in his chair.

MacGillivray's voice spoke in his ear.

'Have I disturbed you?' he asked Love.

'No more than usual. Are you also working on Saturday?'

'We never stop,' said MacGillivray pontifically. 'But I didn't ring to tell you that. I wonder if you could do something for me?'

'I'm busy,' Love told him. 'I'm seeing a patient.'

'This could be medical,' said MacGillivray carefully. 'You could conceivably save a man's life.'

'Go on,' said Love, deliberately not looking at Windsor.

'Here's the situation. One of our people, a double agent during the war, thinks that the other side is on to him.'

'That's a long time ago,' said Love carefully. 'Why should they still be interested in him now?'

'Motives of revenge. And political pride. To show other people who's boss. To persuade - or frighten - doubters and waverers and middle-of-the-liners into coming over to them. I don't want him to fall to the wolves without at least trying to help him.'

'What can I do?'

'Get out your Cord and drive to Minehead, to the caravan site. You'll find a two-tone blue and grey Morris Oxford. I haven't the number. But it's probably the only one there hitched to a caravan.'

'And then?' asked Love. 'Make him an offer for it?'

'No. See the man in the caravan.'

'Why?'

'To help him, of course.'

'How?'

'Get him into a nursing home. It doesn't matter where. We'll pay the bill.'

'What's wrong with him? Is he ill?'

'Not now. Frightened, yes, but ill, I'd say, no. But if someone doesn't take him out of circulation, he could be very ill. Probably dead. And you're the nearest friend I have to him.

'They've tried already to get him at his home, and he rang me. I told him to take off without letting anyone at all know where he was going, and then get in touch when he was at least a hundred and fifty miles out of town.

'He rang me this afternoon. From Minehead.'

'And what did you tell him?'

'That I had a friend, Dr Jason Love, in Bishop's Combe. Only a few miles from where he was speaking. Anyhow, can you hide him somewhere for a couple of days?'

'What use is that out of all eternity?'

'Long enough for us to do some checking on who exactly's tailing him. And why.'

'What's this man look like?' asked Love.

MacGillivray told him.

'There's no need for me to go and see him then,' Love said. 'He's come to see me. You're late.'

'My God,' said MacGillivray. 'He must be scared.'

'Don't invoke the Deity,' said Love irritably. 'You bloody well told him to come and see me.'

'Now, now, doctor,' replied MacGillivray smoothly. 'I don't tell people to do anything. I only make suggestions.'

'Well, I'll make you a suggestion,' said Love. 'Get stuffed. Slowly. With feeling.'

'Some like the feeling,' said MacGillivray placidly 'Does that mean you'll help me?'

'Under the Hippocratic Oath, I try to help everybody who needs my help. Even you.'

He put down the telephone before MacGillivray could reply.

'Now, Mr Windsor,' he said gently. 'Tell me exactly what you're afraid of.'

'You were speaking about me,' said Windsor, his voice tense.

'Yes,' agreed Love. 'Our mutual friend. Colonel MacGillivray.'

'Did he tell you my trouble?' asked Windsor.

'Not really,' said Love. 'Only in general terms. People he tactfully calls the other side are apparently looking for you. Does anyone other than MacGillivray know you've come here?'

Windsor shook his head.

'No-one,' he said. 'When I telephoned the cut-out number to tell MacGillivray, I used a pocket scrambler he'd given me years ago. It's got two sharp spikes to dig into the telephone wires and make an open line secure.'

'A useful gadget. Well, which particular other side is after you now - and why?'

'The Japanese.'

'The Japanese? I didn't know we were fighting them?'

'Not now,' agreed Windsor. 'But this goes back a long way - to when we were. But first, doctor, can I stay here? Or can't you get me in any hospital where I'll be safe?'

'I'll do all I can to help,' said Love carefully. 'I promise you that. But first I must know the trouble.'

He knew that MacGillivray would not have rung him unless there was good reason to believe that Windsor was in real danger, but why from the Japanese?

'To start at the beginning,' said Windsor, 'My mother was Japanese. My father was British - technically, that is. Actually, he was about a quarter Malay. He worked in the telephone exchange. We were left behind in Penang when the Japs invaded in forty-two.

'We could have got away if we'd gone early enough. But we were all so sure the British navy and the army would protect us that, like lots of others, we left it too late.

'Maybe my parents wanted to appear more British than the British, staying at their post until the last, and all that. You know how it is?'

'I know,' said Love gently, imagining the dichotomy of loyalties under stress, seeing the strain of the memory etched on Windsor's unhappy face.

'The Japs shot my father when he was actually at the switchboard. My mother and I were put in a camp. She had diabetes, and the Japanese commandant told me she was a traitor to Nippon and she didn't deserve any special treatment. This meant that she'd die within days unless I worked for them. I spoke Japanese, of course, yet I could pass for a harmless Eurasian. So - I said I'd work.'

'What at?'

'They brought me down to Singapore, and then they let her out. She was allowed to return to our house in Penang, but I had to keep playing my part. The minute I stopped, back she'd go inside. And, with her disease, that meant death.'

'What did you have to do?' asked Love.

'They gave me a portable transmitter. I knew quite a bit about radio even then. I was right down near the Causeway in Singapore, in a room above a Chinese tailor's shop.

'Every night, at different times, I had to radio back on a very short wavelength what the British were doing, where they had set up anti-aircraft guns, even the names of different commanders if I could find them.

'The Japanese used all this over Penang Radio for propaganda purposes. It made them appear all-knowing to the locals. Very effective stuff.'

'And then?' asked Love.

'And then my mother died.'

'How?'

'There was still a black-out in Penang, or a brown-out, or whatever we called it then. One night she fell into a bomb crater, and broke both her legs. She must have lain there for hours in pain. In the morning, she was dead.'

'So what did you do?'

'I heard this from a neighbour of ours who'd fled south, on February the tenth.'

'And Singapore fell five days later?'

'Yes.'

'So?'

'So, I managed to duck out. I'd no-one left to consider but myself. I escaped on a boat to Colombo -probably the last one. And there I gave myself up.'

'To whom?'

'I saw a notice on an office door in a requisitioned house we were all taken to. Field Security Section, it said. There was a sergeant inside. He took me to an officer and then on to someone else, a civilian. I explained I could speak Japanese. But I didn't say I'd been working for them.'

'Understandably.'

'I was passed to various other people, and had all sorts of interviews and tests. Then I was enlisted in the Army and trained in Central India. The usual sort of thing popular then. How to live off the land. What jungle berries were poisonous and which were not. How to kill a man in ten different ways without making a noise. High speed Morse. After nearly a year at this, I parachuted back into Malaya with a radio.

'I stayed there for the rest of the war, and afterwards I gave evidence against several Japanese commanders as war criminals. They were hanged. Then I worked for MacGillivray from time to time. In the Far East, generally. Saigon. Bangkok. Tokyo. Once you've been involved, they never really let you go.'

'When did you marry?'

'In fifty-five. An English nurse. On leave in Ipoh. We had a daughter and then we came to England. My wife didn't like the East much. She thought we'd have a better life here. But we didn't, really. We were just running away from the basic problem - that I wasn't English, and she felt cheated.

'This hadn't mattered so much out there. But it did back here, for her parents never really accepted me. I was just someone their daughter - an only child - had met abroad and foolishly married. Finally, she left me. I came home one evening and found she'd cleared out. With our daughter. I tried to contact her parents, but they'd gone, too.'

He paused.

'So what did you do?'

'What could I do? I told the police, but it was nothing to do with them. Purely a domestic affair, they said. So I went to see a lawyer and he suggested private detectives, but how could I afford their fees? Paying the lawyer was bad enough.

'Anyway, one day I came back from work, and a neighbour, a nosy old woman who lives on her own, said some strangers had been asking about me. I thought my wife might have sent them, so I waited in, hoping they'd turn up again. They did. But they'd nothing to do with my wife.

'They were Japanese. They said they were businessmen, and had known friends of mine - or rather of my mother - in Malaya in the old days. I didn't believe them.'

'What did they want?' asked Love.

'They knew all about me, what I'd done,' said Windsor flatly, his voice sinking to a whisper. 'They were members of some underground military party.

'One said he was the son of a general who'd been executed, largely on my evidence. They said they would kill me, but in their own good time. The most frightening thing was how they said this. Not threateningly, but quite calmly. Like someone explaining he didn't smoke or take sugar in his tea, or something like that.

'After this, nothing for some weeks. Then I started having telephone calls telling me that no matter where I went they would find me. Once or twice, strangers stopped me in the street just to say something like, "The date has been agreed", or, "I wonder if you will be here next week?"

'Before I could reply they'd disappear in the crowd. Then I started to receive newspaper cuttings about people who'd been killed in car crashes in Malaysia, or taken their own lives. I knew one or two of the names. We'd been in the same outfit.'

'Did you go to the police then?'

'No, I rang MacGillivray. He got my line tapped to see if they could find out who was 'phoning, but the calls always came from telephone boxes. By the time they'd traced the number, the caller had rung off.

'Last week, I decided to clear out. I'd had enough. I told MacGillivray I had to get away or go mad. I just couldn't stand the strain any longer. I'd lost nearly two stones in weight. I couldn't sleep properly. He said to tell no-one where I was going; just take the caravan and drive.

'The West Country seemed the best place. I thought no-one would notice one more visitor. So I headed down here.

'I promised to ring him if anyone followed me. I didn't think they would, but last night I came back from the pictures, late, and the fellow in the next caravan knocked at the door and said a couple of men had been to see me. They told him to tell me they'd be back. They asked him to pass this on, no matter when I returned. They said it was important.'

Windsor smiled wryly.

'It was, for I realized I hadn't run away. I'd only run towards them.

'I rang MacGillivray at once, but I couldn't get him. He was out. So I tried again today. He said there wasn't much he could do to help me, but he gave me your name. He said you'd help me if you could. That's why I came here. If I could get into hospital, doctor, I wouldn't be on my own. I'd be in a public ward, with other people. No-one could harm me there.'

'How do you think these fellows followed you to Minehead?' asked Love.

Windsor shrugged.

'I suppose they watched me.'

'Did you drive over here tonight?'

'Yes.'

'Where's your car?'

'Outside the surgery.'

'Drive it into my garage and let's have a look at it.'

Love remembered a visit to Syria when his own car had been followed for miles in darkness across the desert from Damascus(For further details, see 'Passport for a Pilgrim') because someone had given him a packet of cigarettes containing an electronic device that broadcast a tiny repetitive signal. His pursuers had simply tuned in a receiver to the direction from which the signals were strongest, and driven on that bearing.

Windsor followed Love out of the surgery. Love hung the surgery key on a nail just inside the front door of his house and then crossed over to the garage. He switched on the fluorescent lights, and when Windsor had driven the car into the garage, he felt under the mudguards and around the bumpers. Inside the hollow rear right-hand over-rider his fingers touched a small metal cylinder, the size of a pencil-torch battery. He pulled it away easily enough; it was only attached by a small magnet.

'This is how they found you,' he told Windsor. 'You were carrying your own transmitter.'

'My God. To be caught with that old trick! And the number of times I've stuck a bug on a car myself! I never thought of looking.'

He turned it over in his hands.

'Now this is what I suggest,' said Love. 'We'll put it back on your car, and then sooner or later whoever's tracking you will trace you here.'

'And then?' asked Windsor.

'Then I'll take things as they come. In the meantime, you'll be in the loft above the surgery. I've got a camp bed up there, and blankets. I can't get rid of these characters for ever, but I'm sure I can give you a long start on them.'

'A long start. Well, that's something, doctor, and believe me, I'm grateful. But I've still got to go on running away. And I've been running away for a long time. Too long.'

Windsor's voice sounded slack and very tired.

'I'd like to think I could stop running away soon. This isn't just a matter of revenge for them. It's a matter of prestige, a sign of this underground party's growing power. If they can liquidate me after so long, and on the other side of the world, then every other person who might stand in their way will have cause to think again. So they'll get me eventually - if they can.'

'We'll do our best to see they can't,' Love said optimistically, and led him into the waiting room.

Behind a wooden door with an old-fashioned country latch a spiral wooden staircase led up into the loft. He showed Windsor the room, then brought him down to his study and offered him a drink, but he refused.

'I'll drink if we're successful,' he said.

Love poured himself a Masquers, then rang for Mrs Hunter to lay another place for his guest. During supper, Windsor picked at his food, glancing every now and then at the clock on the mantelpiece, and pausing, fork half-way to his mouth, when he heard a car in the lane outside.

Time and again, Love tried to make conversation, but Windsor's mind was so obviously concentrated on his own problems that at first he answered in monosyllables, and finally did not answer at all, but just sat listening. Love told him what he planned to do, but even this could not claim his visitor's close attention.

'I'll need to borrow your wallet,' Love told him. 'And your watch.'

Windsor handed them over without a word. Love put them on a side table.

It was ten o'clock when he showed Windsor to his room up the wooden stairs. He plugged a reading lamp into a wall socket, and pulled the heavy red curtains and weighted them down, where they crossed, with an antique acetylene car headlamp, before he switched on the light.

Love went back to his study, put Windsor's wallet and his watch on the table in front of him, and arranged the curtains so that a gap of light would show to anyone outside. Then he did a little writing, and sat reading, or rather trying to read, his ears alert for the sound of tyres on the drive. He waited longer than he had expected; it was a quarter to one when he heard them.

He put down his book, walked into the hall and shut the study door behind him so that no-one could see him against the light. Then he opened the dining room door, and peered out between the curtains, across the lawn.

Two men were climbing out of a Triumph 2000. They glanced towards the house, saw the light in Love's study through the gap between the curtains, then walked over to Windsor's car. The smaller man put his hand behind the over-rider, and pulled out the metal cylinder. He put this in his jacket pocket, and then they crossed the lawn together, walking in step, the moonlight throwing long shadows behind them as they walked. One pressed the night bell.

Love counted twenty to give himself time to have been disturbed in his study, and then opened the door with a rattling of the check chain. Under the porch light two men of medium height in dark suits stood waiting.

They looked English; and even if they weren't, they certainly were not Japanese. For a moment, Love wondered whether Windsor's terror might have been simulated, part of a mental breakdown, one of the signs of approaching paranoia. Then he remembered MacGillivray's dry Scots voice on the telephone, and the glimpse of the man removing the transmitter from the over-rider.

'I'm sorry to disturb you at this hour, doctor,' that man was saying now, and his voice sounded apologetic, as though he really did regret his visit.

'I'm sorry, too,' said Love, briefly. 'What's the trouble?'

'It's about a friend of ours.'

The man paused.

'What about him?'

'To be frank, doctor, I don't quite know. He's been rather strange in his behaviour for some weeks. You know, odd. Off hand. As though he was terribly worried about something. He's staying on the caravan site near Minehead, and we were all going out to dinner together this evening.

'When he didn't turn up, we went to his van and someone on the site told us that he'd said he was ill and was going to see a doctor. We waited for him to come back, but he didn't turn up, so we rang one or two local doctors, but they knew nothing about him.

'We were very worried by now, so finally we went to the police and the duty sergeant said a man of that description had come in and asked for directions to reach Dr Love's house. So we came on here. I see he's left his car here, doctor. Can you tell us what's happened to him?'

'What's his name?' asked Love.

'Windsor,' replied the second man. 'Like the Castle. He's not at all well. We're really very worried about him.'

'Yes,' said Love. 'Your friend just told me. Please come in.'

They followed him into his study.

'You were right to be concerned about him,' said Love. 'But I'm sorry, it's too late.'

Love pushed a piece of paper across the desk towards them.

'Too late?' the smaller man repeated, his face puckering with surprise.

'I'm sorry to say so. He is now your late friend. Here's his death certificate. Obviously, there'll have to be a post-mortem.'

'He's dead?' said the second man in amazement.

Love pointed to the line, 'Disease or condition directly leading to death,' under which he had written 'heart failure'. In the end, the heart always failed. This description could cover a multitude of deaths.

'Where's the body?'

'I rang the undertaker,' said Love. 'He took it away. He has a chapel of rest. It couldn't very well stay here.'

'What about his belongings?' asked the small man.

Love pointed to Windsor's watch, his wallet.

'That's all he had,' he said.

'Do you mind if we look through the wallet?' asked the first man.

'Do so,' said Love, and pushed it across the desk to him.

The man took out a photograph of a woman with a child about ten, presumably Windsor's wife and daughter: his driving licence, five one-pound notes, an insurance certificate for his car and a receipt for a suit at a dry-cleaner's in Ealing.

'Thank you, doctor,' the man said, replacing all these items in the wallet. 'What a sad ending to an evening. As his closest friend - and in touch with his wife - could we have a copy of the death certificate? She would like to know.'

'Of course.'

Love scribbled on the duplicate form. They read it carefully, and shook hands. Love showed them to the front door.

'Oh, and the undertaker's name, too, please,' the man said, almost as an afterthought. 'We'll have a word with him tomorrow.'

Love had not expected this, so he gave him the number of a director of a local firm who he knew was away on holiday; it might take half a day for them to find they knew nothing about the matter, and every hour counted.

He stood watching them as they drove away. The driver waved back at him through his window. He listened to the beat of the exhaust until it died in the high-banked lanes beyond the village. Then he went back to the study, switched off the light, waited for twenty minutes by his watch and, with the house in darkness, he crossed the drive, and let himself into the waiting room and climbed the stairs.

Love felt pleased with what he had done. They would probably come back, but not for several hours, and by then Windsor would be miles away. He might not have outwitted them permanently, but then life itself was impermanent. At least, he had scored a useful start on his pursuers.

'Mr Windsor,' he called softly.

There was no answer. He opened the door at the top of the stairs, checked that the curtains were pulled, and switched on the reading lamp. Mr Windsor lay under two tartan rugs on the camp bed. On the floor, near his head, a piece of paper was held flat by an ashtray.

Love bent down and felt his pulse, but he knew there would be nothing. The man's wrist looked as thin as a child's. He rolled up one eyelid; Windsor's face was damp and cold to his fingers. Then he picked up the paper.

'Dr Love,' he read. 'Thanks for trying to help me, but I have taken my own way out. I watched the men go away. I waited five minutes and moved the curtains. I really thought they had gone. But, of course, that was naive of me. They had come back on foot and were watching the house, and they saw me.

'I am a coward, doctor, but I am too old to start running again. I went down to your surgery, used your own key, which you will find under my pillow -1 took it from the nail I saw you hang it on inside your front door - and I found a bottle of phenobarb tablets. Then I drank half a pint of brandy. I always carry a pocket flask.

'I have £300 in the Post Office at Ealing. MacGillivray knows my address and where you will find the book. This should be enough to bury me. Buy yourself a bottle of something with the rest, and drink to old days and better days, because the good times are always in the past or the future, but never here and now. Goodbye, and thank you again. I ...'

The letter ended in a scrawl. Windsor must have barely been able to push it under the ash-tray before the drug and the drink produced their deadly reaction.

Love stood up slowly. He suddenly felt immeasurably weary. The challenge of outwitting this man's pursuers had poured its adrenalin through his veins, making him forget his own fatigue. Now he knew that it had all been in vain.

He had thought his plan so clever, yet all he had done was to write out the death certificate for a stranger a few hours in advance. He looked at the certificate he still held in his hand and read the words: 'Other significant conditions contributing to the death, but not related to the disease or condition causing it.'

They would take a long time to list, Love thought, for they went back for more than a quarter of a century, beyond that other Saturday in Singapore, the eve of the city's surrender, when the arteries of an Empire were opened, and centuries of supremacy began to bleed away.

He bent down and pulled the rug over Windsor's face. Its worried look had left it, the wrinkles had all ironed themselves out. He seemed years younger, as he must have looked, Love thought, when he first parachuted over the sleeping jungle long, long ago.

Love walked slowly down the stairs, and stood for a moment in the moonlight, looking across the lawn.

His day had begun with the birth of a child, and had ended with the death of a spy. He thought there should be some moral, some message there, but he couldn't imagine what it might be.

He hoped vaguely that the child would grow up into a happier world, but deep down he knew she wouldn't. There wasn't any happier world; there was only this world. Then he went into the house, and locked the door behind him.

Have you read the other Dr Jason Love casebooks available as e-books?

PASSPORT TO OBLIVION

Passport to Oblivion is the first case book of Dr. Jason Love . . . country doctor turned secret agent. Multi-million selling, published in 19 languages around the world and filmed as *Where the Spies Are* starring David Niven.

'As K pushed his way through the glass doors of the Park Hotel, he realized instinctively why the two stumpy men were waiting by the reception desk. They had come to kill him. ...'

Who was K - and why should anyone kill him? Who was the bruised girl in Rome? Why did a refugee strangle his mistress in an hotel on the edge of the Arctic Circle? And why, in a small office above a wholesale fruiterers in Covent Garden, did a red-haired

Scot sift through filing cabinets for the name of a man he knew in Burma twenty years ago?

None of these questions might seem to concern Dr Jason Love, a country practitioner of Bishop's Combe, Somerset. But, in the end, they all do. Apart from his patients, Dr Love has apparently only two outside interests: his supercharged Cord roadster, and the occasional Judo lessons he gives to the local branch of the British Legion.

But out of the past, to which all forgotten things should belong, a man comes to see him - and his simple, everyday country-life world is shattered like a mirror by a .38 bullet.

"Heir Apparent to the golden throne of Bond" *The Sunday Times*

PASSPORT TO PERIL

Passport to Peril is Dr Jason Love's second brilliant case history in suspense. An adventure that sweeps from the gentle snows of Switzerland to the freezing peaks of the Himalayas, and ends in a blizzard of violence, hate, and lust on the roof of the world. Guns, girls and gadgets all play there part as the Somerset doctor, old car expert and amateur secret agent uncovers a mystery involving the Chinese intelligence service and a global blackmail ring.

"Second instalment in the exploits of Dr Jason Love… Technicolour backgrounds, considerable expertise about weapons… action, driven along with terrific vigour" *The Sunday Times*

"It whips along at a furious pace" *The Sun*

"A great success" *The Daily Express*

PASSPORT IN SUSPENSE

West German submarine 'Seehund' is hijacked during N.A.T.O. manoeuvres in the North Sea. Neo-Nazis want it for a daring operation; seeking out pockets of escaped war criminals in South America, they promise the elderly men free trips home under new identities if they will detonate three atomic devices at carefully positioned points on the sea bed. The subsequent chain reaction will then drastically affect the world's climate, turning both Britain and America into arctic wastelands.

Holidaying in the Bahamas, Dr.Jason Love witnesses at close range the shooting of a beautiful brunette in a speedboat. She had been mistaken for Israeli spy Shamara, assigned to investigate millionaire Paul V.Steyr. Blind and insane, Steyr is the mastermind behind the terrible neo-Nazi plot. Only Love, teamed with Shamara, can stop him...

'The action is supersonic throughout.' *The Guardian*

'A superb example of modern thriller writing at its best' *Sunday Express*

'Third of Dr Love's supercharged adventures... It starts in the sunshine of the Bahamas, swings rapidly by way of a brunette corpse into Mexico, and winds up in the yacht of a megalomaniac ex-Naxi... Action: non-stop: Tension: nail-biting' *Daily Express*

'His ingenuity and daring are as marked as ever' *Birmingham Post*

PASSPORT FOR A PILGRIM

Dr Love's fourth supersonic adventure.

Dr Jason Love is going to attend a medical conference in Damascus and one of his patients asks him to find out how his daughter died in a car accident on the outskirts of Syria's capital. But all is not as it seems. Fulfilling a simple favour turns into a nightmare for the Somerset doctor, turned part-time secret agent...

'Super suspense and, as usual, Love finds a way.' *Daily Express*

'Bullets buzz like a beehive kicked by Bobby Charlton' *Sunday Mirror*

'Action is driven along at a furious pace from the moment the doctor sets foot in Damascus.. a quite ferocious climax. Unputdownable.' *Sheffield Morning Telegraph*

'Thriller rating: High' *The Sun*

IF YOU ENJOYED THIS BOOK WHY NOT TRY:

MANDARIN-GOLD

The first of James Leasor's epic trilogy based on a Far Eastern trading company:

'Highly absorbing account of the corruption of an individual during a particularly sordid era of British imperial history,' *The Sunday Times*

'James Leasor switches to the China Sea more than a century ago, and with pace and ingenuity tells, in novel form, how the China coast was forced to open up its riches to Englishmen, in face of the Emperor's justified hostility' *Evening Standard*

'In the nasty story of opium - European and American traders made fortunes taking the forbidden dope into nineteenth century China, and this novel tells the story of their deadly arrangements and of the Emperor's vain attempts to stop them. Mr. Leasor has researched the background carefully and the detail of the Emperor's lavish court but weak administration is fascinating. The white traders are equally interesting characters, especially those two real-life merchants, Jardine and Matheson.'
Manchester Evening News

This was Robert Gunn's introduction to the China coast. The young Englishman little suspected that he would remember it later as one of the least shocking and least shameful things he had done on his ruthless search for money and power...

It was the year of 1833 when Robert Gunn arrived on the China coast. Only the feeblest of defences now protected the vast and proud Chinese Empire from the ravenous greed of Western traders, and their opening wedge for conquest was the sale of forbidden opium to the native masses.

This was the path that Robert Gunn chose to follow... a path that led him through a maze of violence and intrigue, lust and treachery, to a height of power beyond most men's dreams — and to the ultimate depths of personal corruption.

Here is a magnificent novel of an age of plunder—and of a fearless freebooter who raped an empire.

Robert Gunn stared with stunned surprise at the Oriental merchant whose servants had drugged and brought him to this secluded, incredibly luxurious mansion.

Now his captor offered Gunn the choice between either accepting three thousand British pounds in return for performing a small service, or meeting swift and brutal death.

"What is it that you wish me to do?" Gunn asked as quietly as he could.

"I wish you to make love to my daughter, Mr. Gunn. To mount her, and mount her again, until she is with child by a white man."

THE CHINESE WIDOW

James Leasor's two preceding books in his chronicle of the Far East a century and half ago - FOLLOW THE DRUM and MANDARIN-GOLD were acclaimed by critics on both sides of the Atlantic. THE CHINESE WIDOW is their equal. It combines the ferocious force of the Dutch mercenaries who seek to destroy Gunn's plan; the pathos of a young woman left alone to rule a fierce and rebellious people; the gawky humour of Gunn's partner, the rough, raw Scot MacPherson; the mysterious yet efficacious practice of Chinese medicine, handed on through thousands of years...

When doctors in England pronounced his death sentence, Robert Gunn-founder of Mandarin-Gold, one of the most prosperous Far Eastern trading companies of the nineteenth century-vowed to spend his final year in creating a lasting memorial to leave behind him... to pay back, somehow, his debt to the lands of the East that had been the making of his vast fortune. He had a plan - a great plan - but to see it through he had to confront a fierce and rebellious people, a force of Dutch mercenaries and the Chinese Widow. Who was the Widow? What was her past-and her power...?

Action, suspense and the mysterious splendour of the Orient are combined in this exciting and moving novel.

A FURTHER SELECTION BOOKS BY JAMES LEASOR
AND AVAILABLE AS E-BOOKS
For more details please visit www.jamesleasor.com

BOARDING PARTY

Filmed as *The Sea Wolves,* this is the story of the undercover exploits of a territorial unit. The Germans had a secret transmitter on one of their ships in the neutral harbour of Goa. Its purpose was to guide the U-boats against Allied shipping in the Indian Ocean. There seemed no way for the British to infringe Goa's Portuguese neutrality by force. But the transmitter had to be silenced. Then it was remembered that 1,400 miles away in Calcutta was a source of possible help. A group of civilian bankers, merchants and solicitors were the remains of an old territorial unit called The Calcutta Light Horse. With a foreword by Earl Mountbatten of Burma.

> 'One of the most decisive actions in World War II was fought by fourteen out-of-condition middle-aged men sailing in a steam barge...' - *Daily Mirror*

> 'A gem of World War II history' - *New York Times Book Review*

> 'If ever there was a ready-made film script...here it is' - *Oxford Mail*

GREEN BEACH

In 1942 radar expert Jack Nissenthall volunteered for a suicidal mission to join a combat team who were making a surprise landing at Dieppe in occupied France. His assignment was to penetrate a German radar station on a cliff above 'Green Beach:

Because Nissenthall knew the secrets of British and US radar technology, he was awarded a personal bodyguard of sharp-shooters. Their orders were to protect him, but in the event of possible capture to kill him. His choice was to succeed or die. The story of what happened to him and his bodyguards in nine hours under fire is one of World War II's most terrifying true stories of personal heroism.

> 'Of all the war stories I have read, truth or fiction, this is the best' – Ottawa Journal

> 'Green Beach has blown the lid off one of the Second World War's best-kept secrets' – Daily Express

> 'If I had been aware of the orders given to the escort to shoot him rather than let him be captured, I would have cancelled them immediately' – Lord Mountbatten

> 'Green Beach is a vivid, moving and at times nerve-racking reconstruction of an act of outstanding but horrific heroism' – Sunday Express

> '…a cracking good story' – Globe & Mail

THE RED FORT

James Leasor's gripping historical account of the Indian Mutiny. Described by Cecil Woodham-Smith in the New York Times: "*This is a battle piece of the finest kind, detailed, authentic and largely written from original documents. Never has this story of hate, violence, courage and cowardice been better told.*"

A year after the Crimean War ended, an uprising broke out in India which was to have equal impact on the balance of world power and the British Empire's role in world affairs. The revolt was against the East India Company which, not entirely against its will, had assumed responsibility for administering large parts of India. The ostensible cause of the mutiny sprang from a rumour that cartridges used by the native Sepoy troops were greased with cow's fat and pig's lard — cows being sacred to the Hindus, and pigs abhorred by the Mohammedans. But the roots of the trouble lay far deeper, and a bloody andineptly handled war ensued.

The Red Fort is a breathtaking account of the struggle, with all its cruelties, blunderings and heroic courage. When peace was finally restored, the India we know today began to emerge.

THE MARINE FROM MANDALAY
This is the true story of a Royal Marine wounded by shrapnel in Mandalay in WW2 who undergoes a long solitary march to the Japanese through the whole of Burma and then finds his way back through India and back to Britain to report for duty in Plymouth. On his way he has many encounters and adventures and helps British and Indian refugees. He also has to overcome complete disbelief that a single man could walk out of Burma with nothing but his orders - to report to HQ - and his initiative.

THE MILLIONTH CHANCE
The R101 airship was thought to be the model for the future, an amazing design that was 'as safe as houses ... except for the millionth chance'. On the night of 4 October 1930 that chance in a million came up, however. James Leasor brilliantly reconstructs the conception and crash of this huge ship of the air with compassion for the forty-seven dead - and only six survivors.

> 'The sense of fatality grows with every page ... Gripping' - *Evening Standard*

THE ONE THAT GOT AWAY

Franz von Werra was a Luftwaffe pilot shot down in the Battle of Britain. The One that Got Away tells the full and exciting story of his two daring escapes in England and his third and successful escape: a leap from the window of a prisoners' train in Canada. Enduring snow and frostbite, he crossed into the then neutral United States. Leasor's book is based on von Werra's own dictated account of his adventures and makes for a compelling read.

THE PLAGUE AND THE FIRE

This dramatic story chronicles the horror and human suffering of two terrible years in London's history. 1665 brought the plague and cries of 'Bring Out Your Dead' echoed through the city. A year later, the already decimated capital was reduced to ashes in four days by the fire that began in Pudding Lane. James Leasor weaves in the first-hand accounts of Daniel Defoe and Samuel Pepys, among others.

> 'An engrossing and vivid impression of those terrible days' - *Evening Standard*

> 'Absorbing ... an excellent account of the two most fantastic years in London's history' - *Sunday Express*

WHO KILLED SIR HARRY OAKES?

James Leasor cleverly reconstructs events surrounding a brutal and unusual murder. It is 1943 and Sir Harry Oakes lies horrifically murdered at his Bahamian mansion. Although a self-made multi-millionaire, Sir Harry is an unlikely victim -- there are no suggestions of jealousy or passion. Leasor makes the daring suggestion that Sir Harry Oakes' murder, the burning of the liner Normandie in New York Harbour in 1942 and the Allied landings in Sicily are all somehow connected.

'The story has all the right ingredients - rich occupants of a West Indian tax haven, corruption, drugs, the Mafia, and a weak character as governor' - *Daily Mail*

Books by James Leasor and becoming available as ebooks. Please visit www.jamesleasor.com for details on all these books or contact info@jamesleasor.com for more information on availability. Follow on Twitter: **@jamesleasor** for details on new releases.

Jason Love novels
Passport to Oblivion (filmed, and republished in paperback, as Where the Spies Are)
Passport to Peril (Published in the U.S. as Spylight)
Passport in Suspense (Published in the U.S. as The Yang Meridian)
Passport for a Pilgrim
A Week of Love
Love-all
Love and the Land Beyond
Frozen Assets
Love Down Under

Jason Love and Aristo Autos novel
Host of Extras

Aristo Autos novels
They Don't Make Them Like That Any More
Never Had A Spanner On Her

Robert Gunn novels
Mandarin-Gold
The Chinese Widow
Jade Gate

Other novels
Not Such a Bad Day
The Strong Delusion
NTR: Nothing to Report

Follow the Drum
Ship of Gold
Tank of Serpents

Non-fiction
The Monday Story
Author by Profession
Wheels to Fortune
The Serjeant-Major; a biography of R.S.M. Ronald Brittain, M.B.E., Coldstream Guards
The Red Fort
The One That Got Away
The Millionth Chance: The Story of The R.101
War at the Top (published in the U.S. as The Clock With Four Hands)
Conspiracy of Silence
The Plague and the Fire
Rudolf Hess: The Uninvited Envoy
Singapore: the Battle that Changed the World
Green Beach
Boarding Party (filmed, and republished in paperback, as The Sea Wolves)
The Unknown Warrior (republished in paperback as X-Troop)
The Marine from Mandalay
Rhodes & Barnato: the Premier and the Prancer

As Andrew MacAllan (novels)
Succession
Generation
Diamond Hard
Fanfare
Speculator
Traders

As Max Halstock
Rats – The Story of a Dog Soldier

Printed in Great Britain
by Amazon